The Fifth Di...
December 2023

Features
42   *Becoming Jade* Reviewed by Lisa Timpf
74   *Everything Everywhere All at Once* Reviewed by Lee Clark Zumpe
112   Who's Who

Novelette
46   The Healer's Apprentice by Jason Lairamore

Short Stories
11   Fall of the Dark God by Mike Adamson
28   The Dark by Randall Andrews
77   She Makes Narcissus Bloom by Lisa Voorhees
92   Rattling Bones on the Black River by Ethan Robles

Flash Fiction
37   The Happy Harper Home by Glen R. Stripling
69   Woman in the Moon by Terrie Leigh Relf

Poetry
27   Alien Rose by Guy Belleranti
36   Tanka by Tyree Campbell
40   It Wasn't Silly Putty by Terrie Leigh Relf
68   Life by Angela Acosta

Illustrations
41   Nuclear Insect by Denny Marshall
45   Beautiful Death by Sandy DeLuca

THE STAFF OF THE FIFTH DI...:

EDITOR: Tyree Campbell
WEBMASTER: David Blalock
COVER DESIGNERS: Laura Givens; Marcia A. Borell

Cover art "The Negotiator" by Laura Givens
Cover design by Laura Givens

Vol. IV, No.3   December 2023

The Fifth Di... is published three times a year on the 1st day of April, August, and December in the United States of America by Hiraeth Publishing, P.O. Box 1248, Tularosa, NM, 88352. Copyright 2023 by Hiraeth Publishing. All rights revert to authors and artists upon publication except as noted in selected individual contracts. Nothing may be reproduced in whole or in part without written permission from the authors and artists. Any similarity between places and persons mentioned in the fiction or semi-fiction and real places or persons living or dead is coincidental. Writers and artists guidelines are available online at www.hiraethsffh.com. Guidelines are also available upon request from Hiraeth Publishing, P.O. Box 1248, Tularosa, NM, 88352, if request is accompanied by a self-addressed #10 envelope with a first-class US stamp. Editor: Tyree Campbell.

A Little Help, Please

In the world of the small indie press we fight a never-ending battle for attention to our work, as writers and in publishing. Here's an example: big publishers [you know who they are] have gobs of $$$ that they can devote to advertising and marketing. Here at Hiraeth Publishing, our advertising budget consists of the deposits for whatever soda bottles and aluminum cans we can find alongside the highways. Anti-littering laws make our task even more difficult . . . ☺

That's where YOU come in. YOU are our best promoter. YOU are the one who can tell others about us. Just send 'em to our website, tell them about our store. That's all. Just that.

Of course, we don't mind if you talk us up. We're pretty good, you know. We have some award-winning and award-nominated writers and artists, plus other voices well-deserving to be heard [not everyone wins awards, right?] but our publications are read-worthy nevertheless.

That number once again is:
        www.hiraethsffh.com

Friend us on Facebook at Hiraeth Publishing
Follow us on Twitter at @HiraethPublish1

Pevely Keiser in:
THE IPHAJEAN LARK

Five hundred years into the future, Pevely Keiser is the capo of the criminal organization called Temmen. Temmen runs itself, for the most part, with only a few nudges from Pevely to keep people in line. Lately she has two things on her mind. She wants to do something good and useful with the funds that accrue to the gang. And she wants a companion or two to help her…and perhaps to share her bed, for she well knows it's lonely at the top.

In the process of training her two new assistants (and possible companions) Pevely comes across a young woman being chased. Taking her on board, Pevely soon learns of a devastating conspiracy that threatens the Confederation with totalitarian rule. The key to the solution lies in the hands of one of her employees, but is it the right key? Only the corporate hierarch who leads the conspiracy knows for sure. And he is the father of the woman Pevely rescued.

https://www.hiraethsffh.com/product-page/iphajean-lark-by-tyree-campbell

New from Hiraeth Publishing!!
The Spark
By Stephen C. Curro

Katrina grew up in a frigid world ruled by a tyrant. By day, she works as a mechanic. At night, she becomes the Ace, the King's personal assassin. She's not proud of her job, but she's accepted that it's the way things are. At least she has her boyfriend Dez and his little brother Uriah to light her life.

When Katrina is ordered to quash a rebel attack on the King's Command Center, she thinks it's just another job. But as she uncovers the plot, she is shocked to learn that Dez may be involved with the dissidents. Now Katrina must make an impossible choose— eliminate the one she loves, or defy the King she swore to serve.

The Spark is a sci-fi thriller about love, betrayal, and how the futures of others, even a whole civilization, can be determined through a single choice.

https://www.hiraethsffh.com/product-page/the-spark-by-stephen-c-curro

The Oculist's Daughter
By Angel Favazza

The Oculist's Daughter by Angel Favazza is a steampunker in the old west. It's got a semi-mad scientist (her dad), her, of course, plus outlaws, Indians, Wyoming, a poison gas for killing natives, and an Indian guide. It all adds up to a rollicking adventure.

https://www.hiraethsffh.com/product-page/oculist-s-daughter-by-angel-favazza

Living Bad Dreams
By Denise Hatfield

When dreams come alive, there's no telling where they will lead. Everything changes when you realize that, dream or no dream, you're going to die. What do you do then?

Type: Novella
Audience: adults
Ordering Link:
Print Edition ($9.00):
https://www.hiraethsffh.com/product-page/living-bad-dreams-by-denise-hatfield-1

ePub edition ($2.99):
https://www.hiraethsffh.com/product-page/living-bad-dreams-by-denise-hatfield-2

Feed Me Wicked Things
By Lee Clark Zumpe

There is tremendous power in words, and few writers can draw upon that power better than Lee Clark Zumpe. In "Feed Me Wicked Things" he summons topics ranging from the poignant horror of Srebrenica in the 1990s to the lynching trees of the 1890s, from the futility of assassination to the thoughts of a lonely passing. Evocative and provocative, Zumpe once read cannot be forgotten.

https://www.hiraethsffh.com/product-page/feed-me-wicked-things-by-lee-clark-zumpe

Fall of the Dark God
Mike Adamson

The priest Zareft sat beside the highroad that led west through the shallowing hills of Avestium, snaked through groves and hamlets, down through the ring of barrier mountains to the Inland Sea, which sparkled in blue vista below the afternoon sun.

None would have known Zareft and none would examine him closely, for he wore the threadbare raiment of a beggar and a rough-hewn staff lay across his knees. A hood concealed his features — the eyes that saw all — but no beggar's bowl sat at his side. The king did not forbid those without means to beg in Avestium, and nor would his soldiers molest them. But upon this road the stern-faced, mailed Guards of the Temple practiced their own law, and the tribute in the pockets of pilgrims flowed west without diversion.

In Zareft's day the Temple Guards were merely a ceremonial force, but in later years he was often tempted to spit upon their heels. He had held his bile, though, and bided his time, for there were things that must be done and his life was not a brass coin, to be disposed of cheaply.

Now it was the Year of the Ram, therefore the ninth cycle since the advent of the Great God Sho'Tan. Zareft recalled the night when He was born into the world in a ball of flame which moved across the heavens, trailing fire and a scorching wind that shook houses and bent trees in the high country. He had plunged into the Inland Sea, which seethed and boiled near the point of impact for more than a day.

Then, Zareft was but a priestling in the worship of the Sunhawk and the sacred Stag of the Moon; and they were good days, in the cloistered peace of the great temple at the summit of the awesome spire of rock which rose from the Inland Sea. The sheer islet was connected to the mainland by a bridge of stone, built over the generations by two dynasties of Avestian kings. But then the star fell, and the High Priests labored to divine its significance.

In fear of world's end they probed the lake, and Zareft remembered the day when something was brought, cold and rancid, to the island. Long days passed behind closed doors and there were whisperings among the monks — that something not of the Earth had been given harbor.

But young monks were not privy to the doings of high office, and days became weeks. Finally the king's messengers would no longer be placated, and demanded pronouncement on the matter. At last all was revealed, and heralds rode throughout Avestium and to kingdoms beyond: Kharthos to the south, Sarepan upon the eastern sea, Lymnos in the archipelagos of the west, Thule in the tundra'd northland. They carried word that a new face of God was opened to mankind, a synthesis of sun and moon come down into the world to receive the tribute of the seasons; and they called upon every living soul to make pilgrimage to the Inland Sea, to look upon the Celestial One.

In the private cloisters of the abbot, the monks whispered, sat a divine being, an entity sent down by the Great Mystery to guide humankind's path into uncertain tomorrows. In orderly groups monks, priests and novices were led before the Eminence. Zareft recalled every detail of the day when he and his classmates visited the abbot's garden and bowed their shaven heads before a marble arbor in which sat something beyond description.

A golden robe had been trimmed around its bulk, obscuring all but the vaguest impressions, and Zareft observed those about him as much as the Eminence. They were afraid, some trembling, some whispering their mantras as the abbot stood to one side, hands folded in his saffron robe, a benign smile creasing his old face as if he had seen the gates of heaven thrown wide.

Abbot Ku'an Far was a great and learned scholar for whom Zareft had the deepest respect, and his calm and serious air assured the young priest there was no danger. Zareft looked more closely at the Eminence and was struck at once — no matter how cleverly a robe was cut, it could not conceal the fact that what it covered was not human. Though the Eminence barely moved and made no sound, Zareft was sure he caught the glitter of eyes within the shadowed hood. The shoulders seemed too broad, the head too low; the sleeves meeting over a capacious girth were filled not with arms but with some members which served in lieu.

These impressions had stayed with Zareft when the monks were passed out of the sanctum, and for all his days to come; for it was the only time he set eyes upon what the world would come to call the Great God Sho'Tan. Each night he dreamed of the being who domiciled in the abbot's apartments and a vague fear churned in him, waking him every few hours. There was nothing here of the serene worship of sun and moon, nothing of the calm beauty of hawk and stag. Zareft would lie in the darkness of his cell and whisper his mantras, take control of body and mind and marshal his thoughts.

By day he fed the hawks in the Sun Temple, groomed the reindeer in their sacred byres, and he listened to the whispers of the monks at their meal, or in the Grand Library where priests transcribed old papyrus for new. The peace of the island was tainted by a terrible presence, and many were the eyes that looked up to the terraces and walls of the abbot's offices. Something was not right. Zareft had felt it deep in his soul and shared his suspicions with others. They muttered at their work, and their seniors did not reprimand them.

Emissaries of the kings came upon the Inland Sea of Avestium as the new moon settled in the west. Rich merchants — eager not to be judged harshly in the next world for the disposition of their wealth in this — laid tribute before the god: a carpet of gold and silver which they bade the Eminence use to further His work upon the Earth.

But as the pilgrims began their march the sweet airs of the isle began to fade, replaced by something sinister; a gray cloud settled over the monastery as the priests sensed ever more that the Eminence was not the divinity it had at first seemed. The mystic knowledge said to have been given to the high council of priests in those first weeks appeared increasingly sacrilegious. Transcripts were deemed too dangerous for common hands, and the abbot labored to produce an edition for general monastic consumption; but those close to him told of a weakness, a lethargy, an illness coming upon him. He slept often, and was wasting in body.

They also whispered of the Eminence. It was growing; it

allowed no human eye to fall upon its form; it murmured in sibilant hissings when alone, and its voice became a deep and hollow rushing when it addressed those who served it. They said its appetite was bottomless — it consumed the rations of five men per day, and demanded more.

A day came when Zareft and his fellow priests saw little if any divinity in the Eminence, and determined to seek audience with the abbot. They would request clarification of its status, and how it reflected upon the established faith. But time had marched by them and their courage was mocked by the tolling of the great bronze bell of the Sun Tower. The abbot was stricken and the priests were ordered to his side to pay their last respects.

In his simple bed the abbot lay, thin and pale. A deathly pallor sunk his eyes in waxy skin, and with listless orbs he watched the lines of tearful monks as they filed through his chamber. Sometimes an old friend shared a moment's silence with him in solitude. Upon his turn to enter, Zareft found the guard holding the column, and he was passed in alone.

Sandals silent upon the carpeted tiles, Zareft knelt at the bedside and whispered a prayer for the abbot, sensing as he did that they were not in private. Some great presence hovered beyond a curtained doorway; some perception hounded his thoughts, and he shut it out with a swift mantra and mudra. Before his eyes the abbot roused, lifted a hand to move his blanket, revealing a scroll; the ends were gold-bound with the hawk crest, which defined it as the Sacred Scroll of the Sun, the central doctrine of the faith. With trembling fingers he pressed it to Zareft, tugging at his robe to tell him silently, he must conceal it. Then the young priest rose, clutching his ambiguous gift, and backed with bowed head to the door. He looked up once to see a fond smile on the abbot's lips.

Leaving the vigil, Zareft returned to his cell, took out the scroll and unrolled it reverently. It was the standard text, but in the margins were inscribed the calligraphic letters of the mystic writings of Menoreth. These were the sigils of greatest power, the highest invocations of honor and the benign beauty of truth; and they were a guarded language of priests. Hurrying to the Grand Library, he took from its case the bronze-bound Book of Menoreth, reacquainted himself with the characters — and as he read, realized the abbot had given him a warning of the most terrible urgency.

Sitting in the deserted library, he warred with his conscience. Did the Eminence know the abbot had at last penetrated its mighty veil of darkness, thrown up to ward off his all-sensing mind? Did it realize a young priest knew the truth — that no divinity imbued its flesh, and its awesome knowledge alone did not win it devotion and worship?

Should he inform the prior? At once, surely, he thought; but before he could move a thin scream drifted over the monastery, followed by a booming roar such as the world had never heard. Returning the book to its case, Zareft ran to the courtyards and found the abbot dead upon the flagstones. From above came a wailing of priests, that the old man had risen from his bed with an upsurgance of energy, crossed to his terrace and plunged forth of his own free will, a smile of triumph written boldly on his tired face.

The roar of the unseen entity — redolent with base, animal anger, cunning and brutality unmasked in the sound — stopped the island in its tracks. For long moments the monks looked up at the garden above. Then something moved within Zareft, some tide of revulsion, and he turned to run, seeing others similarly smitten. He made for the walls that looked down upon the evening sea. The moon hung low in the west, and as a second terrible roar brayed across the mountain he ran on for the gate houses. They guarded the winding path up the steep slopes from the rocky beaches and landing stage, by the confluence of the causeway.

In the twilight he saw ceremonial guards staring transfixedly up the mountain, and felt as their souls were taken in a slimy grasp. Something foul descended like a death shroud over the island as a power out of control raced to overtake his fleeing footsteps. Only the sacred scroll within his robe kept his mind clear, the faith in Hawk and Stag as the good avatars of the Earth telling him he must resist the terror from the sky.

He rushed headlong from the gates, down the perilous incline to the shore. At each stage the guards and travelers were stricken in their wonder, dumbfounded, hands frozen in ritual gesture to ward evil. Zareft ran as if his life were ending. An unspeakable, morbid fascination called him back, whispering of the wonders awaiting one who dared tread a forbidden path; and as his pace slowed, incredibly, against his will, he ran onto the bridge.

Burning cressets lit its fantastic length, away toward the horizon, and no pilgrim was near enough to see as the young priest fought his deepening surrender to the languor which locked each soul in its thrall. Convulsive steps took him to the parapet and he pitched headlong to the cool waters below. The last thought in his mind was that if death was the only escape, the price was surely not too high.

The Great God Sho'Tan was born into the world more upon that day than when the star had fallen. The star awoke a course of events, but upon the abbot's passing the Eminence reached out and took black control of its world, and Zareft could thank only the Sunhawk that his fall into the sea jarred him to his senses. He swam beneath the bridge as night thickened, then climbed up by a fisherman's stage to the roadway.

He never looked back upon the mystic isle, knowing in his soul that Sho'Tan was no god, but a destroyer. If all other priests of the Hawk and the Stag were ensnared in its evil coils, it devolved upon him alone to drive the being from its tower, strike it down from its vantage of worship and deceit, and reawaken the true faith.

How he would do these things, he knew then, would command the remainder of his life.

*　　*　　*

The Eminence came among men and Zareft fled his home upon the Inland Sea in the Year of the Lion. The frightened young man hid by day and moved by night, fearing some report of a robed priest would filter back to the isle; but as the days passed he conquered these thoughts. He knew little of the outside world, and must learn by observation as he trekked the long road to Lymnos in the west. He had studied the texts of that kingdom and knew enough of its history and customs to feel less alien there than elsewhere.

To move quietly and unknown, he was forced to the theft of a wayfarer's robe from the stocks of a merchant caravan. In payment he left an armful of sweet roots, which must surely be worth some measure of one's labor. With a hood concealing his shaven head and a staff of yew wood in hand, he trod the dusty road to the sunset and determined to stand outside of life. To watch, learn and, when the time was right, make his way back to ancient Avestium and carry out his ultimate duty.

* * *

All this was distant memory to Zareft now, as he sat beside the highroad to the Inland Sea, his beggar's attire earning him privacy. Nine years was an age, and he was no longer the priestly youth who fled the fall of darkness. No razor had touched his scalp since that time, and his hair fell thickly past his shoulders. The hands so accustomed to work in the temple long ago turned their skills to other applications: he had cut wood and built for those without the knowledge, helped heal the sick and shepherd the poor.

But also, he learned the ways of weapons in the seas of Lymnos, in their endless war with pirate galleys from the unknown ocean beyond. The agility and fleet-handed skills of the priest were soon crowned by the survival instincts of an adventure which all but cost him the path of his duty in a pointless waste of life.

Zareft revered life in all its forms and had never let flesh pass his lips in all his years in the world. But the greatest needs of life fell upon him, and he became a warrior — a wandering swordsman of many names, to whom the hawks would come inexplicably, making common folk bow their heads in wonder and remember the old days ... before the coming of Sho'Tan.

Great was the power of Sho'Tan, and great His fear. Should a harvest fail it was because He was displeased. Should famine or disease walk abroad, the God was angered. Zareft had heard the tales, had stood with others to listen when the heralds made proclamation on behalf of the new abbot, in the name of God and king.

On the first day of the Year of the Bull, it was made law that a tithe would be paid by all farmers and merchants, all villages and towns, to the Temple of Sho'Tan; and this was enforced by the Guards. Now the pilgrims labored to the Inland Sea laden with grain, corn and honey, with silk and spice and gold. The temple grew fat; the booming voice of the Great God echoed over the island. Pilgrims returned to their lands blanched and quiet, not quick to speak of their observances.

When pressed, they told of a foul air, and said the God now resided in the Sun Temple itself, veiled from men's eyes by curtains of silk which blew gently in the wind from the sea. They spoke of silent priests with eyes like cold flame, wasted men who labored to record taxes and tribute; they said the island was a prison and the Guards rode the Pilgrim's Road day and night, hanging thieves and driving out beggars.

In the Year of the Balances the tithe was doubled, and in the Year of the Archer it was increased to thrice its initial figure, the extra to be paid in foodstuffs. Now the peasants must till the land for the Temple one day in three, and they appealed to the king in vain. He was powerless; a cold terror in his heart stayed him from sending his soldiers to right the injustice. Who was he, mere man, to defy the Great God Sho'Tan, a Celestial Being?

Frantic curses were breathed upon the God, the temple banners were spat upon or stamped into the ground, and vigorous were the guards in putting down such dissent. As the seasons ground by, the lifeblood of the kingdom disappeared into the isle, and fearful tales were told in the dark: that the God had ordered beasts of the field brought before it, likewise criminals and the condemned. Heretics were high upon this list, receiving divine judgment — and were never seen again. Horror beyond all reckoning was attributed to the God, and all perversions to his followers. The Hawk and the Stag were forgotten symbols of an age of reason, and secret masses were said by lay-preachers to their honor.

* * *

In the Year of the Fishes Zareft, mounted and clothed in leather and fine flax, crossed the frontier into Avestium and made his way by the Pilgrim's Road toward the Inland Sea. By now a tall, broad-shouldered man, he carried the weapons of his trade: a bow at his shoulder, a shield at his side, a sword wrapped in sheepskin by his saddle. He melted into the countryside, a nameless wanderer, and vanished from sight to build a cabin in the wild, wooded hills above the sea, and bide his time. He reached out with his senses to the tower, blue with distance, where the Eminence squatted in its repulsiveness, felt the probing waves of insensate hunger, and shielded himself with mystic sign and mantra.

  The warrior knew a way to gain entrance to the tower which would not draw guards upon him, but it would take months of careful planning. As the Fishes gave way to the Water-Bearer, and he to the Ram, and the world shook itself free of winter, Zareft made his preparations. He observed those on the Pilgrim's Road, watched the merchants and freemen, heralds and soldiers, foreigners and courtiers — and knew, as the first harvest of spring was gathered, the time had come.

* * *

The sun slanted toward the west, outlining the tower like a devil's finger as Zareft rose by the roadside and made his way home to the woods. As he passed beyond sight of the traffic he straightened his back, threw off the hood and quickened his pace.

  When the first stars shone in the purple twilight he stepped into his rough cabin and was greeted by the flicker of the hearth fire and the bold green eyes of Freja, the woman he had taken to wife this past year. She knew he was a man driven by a mission but she asked no questions, and for this he loved her very much. As a young priest he had never taken his final vows, but he felt deeply that they would have meant little here. Freja gave him what he had never known in any other woman on his travels, and he believed her to be a foreshadowing of the life's task which was so near at hand.

  That night, when the moon rode above the trees, Zareft made the signs of reverence and repeated the devotions to the Horned One, a silent whisper as he stood in the chill air, axe in hand, to bring in wood from the block. With a deep resolve he put the future into its place and shut out the past. He went inside and barred the door; he stoked the fire and lay down with his woman, to feast upon her red hair and ample beauty in the flicker of the flames. When they were done, they rested in the blankets and furs, one last contented night.

  He lay awake, Freja curled in his arms as the sun's first rays inched over the trees and dust motes danced in the air. The warrior priest murmured an ancient incantation, fingers upraised in a handsign, and stroked his wife's cheek. She slept deep and sound as he slid out of bed and wrapped her warmly; then he traced a powerful sigil upon her forehead with his finger, repeating the words that would keep her sleeping for the next two whole days and nights. He paused to look down upon her with a fondness which tore his heart, and hoped he would come back to her. Perhaps he would not be able.

Dressed in the leather and flaxcloth of a wandering swordsman, Zareft took his weapons from their hiding place, oiled and polished them — slid home sword, knife, axe, bow and shafts, shield and *shuriken*. He tied back his hair with a strip of leather and bound on his boots. With ritual gestures he barred the door subtly before he made his way to the byre among the trees, where his horse was stabled. He fed and saddled her, swung a leg over her broad back, and took rein to fade into the morning mist which clothed the green forest.

In the silence of the woods it was hard to think that evil walked abroad in the world, and in all his years Zareft had come to realize good and evil were relative values. One was meaningless without the other, and it was one's destined place to resist — or commit — evil. The earth was good, this he knew.

A bubbling stream flowing down to the sea was cool and clear, and he let the horse drink and rest a moment before they moved on, shapes amongst the trees. Skirting the shore of the Inland Sea, he rode most of the day, eating from his saddlebags on the move. It was a long way to the small cove he knew and he rested the horse, sometimes walking by her side on the woodland trail, pausing to let her graze for a while before coaxing her on with a whistle and a stroke.

The sun was sinking over the barrier mountains when he rode down a long, tree-lined defile beside a sluggish river which emptied into the sea at a rocky, sand-and-gravel strewn cove. There, he tethered the horse on a grassy shoulder where she could graze within reach of water.

Zareft lay down to rest, eat and drink. The colors of sunset painted the world, the shadows of the mountains reached across the sea and the last light of the sun rose up the distant spire of rock to the temple, like the holy hawks of the day. At last he drew the small boat he had constructed from its concealment under a thicket of briarwood.

Checking it over in the last light, he placed his weapons aboard, bade farewell to the horse and pushed the craft out into the river flow. He rowed into midstream as he drifted out past sand bars where wading birds squabbled over shellfish. Clearing the shore, he hauled up a sail of woven grass cords. He tied it off and set the tiller on a course for the distant isle.

The warrior could have walked in with the pilgrims across the causeway, but there was no way to conceal his weapons, nor avoid arousing suspicion when he must depart from the devotions of the crowd. It was better to enter unseen, and to do so he had one choice.

He could not swim beneath the causeway, it was much too far; so he must approach from the opposite side of the tower, where the Guards would be least alert. The third option — he might overcome a Guard, take his polished brass and silk uniform and enter boldly amongst their ranks — was abhorrent. Too many ills were attributed to those colors for him to usurp them even for a moment, nor for any reason.

It would be a long night for Zareft. He watched the stars brighten overhead and kept the rising giant over his bow while the horned one and the seven sisters climbed up by the mast. He skimmed on in the silence of the calm sea, a whisper in the darkness, and before midnight the waning moon rose in a wash of orange light, silhouetting the island. Now he saw the flicker of cressets high upon the spire, where the monastery's towers rose to their supreme heights, and soon he heard the wash of the sea against its stony base.

He was approaching from the west side and knew the rocks were steepest here. No fishermen came to this part of the great lake, as the sewerage outfall of the monastery made for poor catches; the main outlet pipes issued at the base of the cliff on the opposite side from the causeway. Nearby was a rarely-used maintenance platform. The spring storms were seldom able to damage the bronze pipes from cisterns in the living rock, vessels which were washed constantly by seawater lifted by rotating wheels.

As he neared the stony spire Zareft checked closely that the outlet station was deserted and, satisfied all was quiet, rowed in. A rough ledge served as jetty, and he tied on at a bronze ring bolted to the ancient rock. Climbing onto the ledge, he checked the time against the stars, and from the boat took a coil of hemp rope with a lead weight at its end. He could have gone up the service way by the pipeline, but great bronze doors were locked there, barred and guarded. He had long since determined that the best way was the one least defended.

The island rose against the stars like a black titan and Zareft, feeling like an ant at its feet, braced himself. With all gear secured, he took hold of the first ledge and began to climb: a long and agonizing ascent, rock to rock, outcrop to outcrop, up salt-lichen encrusted boulders where fractured slabs lay canted outward and storms had loosened shale and gravel. Here he murmured the hawk mantras to keep resting seabirds asleep; young ones on nests deep in the clefts reminded him that life's miracle was perpetual, even here on the brink of the greatest horror the world had known since the Age of Chaos.

The wind blew about him as the roll of the sea diminished, and as the bull neared zenith he found himself at a gentle incline which he scaled quickly, tracing a way about the curve of the spire. Then he climbed again, higher and higher, until at last he reached a wall of moss-grown stone blocks, an ancient foundation of the monastery, probably over a thousand years old. As his hands touched it he felt a warmth — a vibration that seemed to say a son had come home to set the house to rights — and he moved on, climbing now with the ease of a goat where the blocks formed a worn stair.

New strength imbued his muscled arms. When he finally reached a grassy bluff and could look down across the rocks at the roofs and gardens of the monastery, he felt a wide resolve. At this height, surpassed only by the highest Towers of Retreat, he could see the firefly lights on the bridge running ruler straight across the dark sea toward the faint corona of the town, which had grown up on the shore to serve the pilgrims in their endless journey.

Now came the trial, the final run. Below him, somewhere in the monastery, a black heart of evil festered and his life's work was to cut it out. The walls of the upper terraces lay close by, and he listening at the foot to catch the tread of guards before using the rope to scale the well-maintained smoothness of dressed stone. At the top he coiled the line about his waist, strung an arrow to his bow and crept toward the inner gardens.

The Eminence grumbled in its slumber, a sound like distant thunder, and a sense of corruption hung over the monastery. Zareft saw no one moving except for guards patrolling the wall. They were lazy, some were drunk, and he avoided them with ease, gaining the inner courtyards. Now, overwhelming waves of memory washed in on him with terrible strength: visions of this place as it had once been, the sanctuary where he grew up and learned his values. He had no wish to defile it with his actions, and was sure that when he raised his hand it would be to clean the mire from this castle.

Again the Eminence stirred and a flash of lightning crossing Zareft's mind. *It knows.* As if at a stroke, the monastery shook itself awake and doors opened. Shaven-headed monks, gaunt faced, with sunken eyes and the corrupt and wasted bodies of the undead, stepped out into the starlight; guards came from their posts and swords were drawn.

Now Zareft was the warrior. He drew bead to send shafts through the breastplates of guard after guard as he made a swift run through the neglected gardens, toward the confluence of passages below the Sun Temple. The Eminence was awake — its voice rumbled out over the rooftops. Pilgrims encamped below, waiting for the gates to be opened at sunrise, cowered in their tents and sleeping bags, whimpering in fear.

With his last arrow gone Zareft laid aside his bow and drew the great steel sword from its baldric. He kissed the hawk-engraved blade and took the double hilt in hand below the staghorn crosspiece, drew a breath and whirled from cover. A rank of guards barred the great doors to the temple and he laid into them, sword a wheel of light against the darkness, striking blue sparks as it met the naked steel of their blades or bit the stone at their backs.

At once he knew these men had always had the roaring giant as their backbone; the people's fear of Sho'Tan was the guards' greatest ally. They were good at hanging peasants but had never been challenged by swordsmen of quality. They had their own fear of the Eminence, however, and fought with all their might, calling for assistance before falling in bloodied tatters, a heap of corpses at the doors of the holy shrine.

Those iron-bound rosewood portals were barred from within, and Zareft climbed the stone walls to a high window which backed a gallery. Drawing his rope inside, he slipped through as boots thudded in the passageway.

Looking down from the gallery in dim torchlight, he took his <u>shuriken</u> and in lightning flicks sent them scything into the guards who stood, and died, by the door. Then he ran for a stairway letting down upon the main floor. The temple where he had once venerated the hawks was bell-shaped, and at its apex a crystal refracted the light of sun and moon across a zodiacal map of ebony and alabaster which covered the floor.

But this was now shrouded — a great red silk curtain encircled the inner part of the chamber, some fifty feet across. Zareft went forward slowly, sword in hand, between stacks of tribute. A case of gold lay open among barrels of corn and oil, rich silk. As much as the feeling of evil made him sick, it disgusted him to see a holy place turned into a warehouse.

Pausing, hand upon the curtain, he recalled the creature in the abbot's gardens so long ago, and gripped his sword tighter. There was no god here. Great it may be, but it was as mortal as himself, and it had taken the part of darkness. He drew the curtain aside and found a ring of torches within, illuminating a pit. The entire floor of the temple was gone and a yawning abyss greeted him, from which issued a faintly putrid odor. A golden rail encircled the pit, broken at one point by a stage, and the stonework below was cut to resemble blocks.

Making himself look downward, Zareft at first saw nothing; but then his eyes made out a shapeless mass at the bottom, and abruptly a volcanic roar came up at him. He staggered back from it as a wave of sickening air washed up the wall; then the mass moved, a part rose up, and witchfires shone deep in black hollows while a maw gaped like the door to hell. Multiple members writhed across the immobile body

— it lay like a beached and helpless sea creature, and it called out in words unknown to Zareft.

Guards were hammering at the door with spear butts and they would soon scale a wall to enter. Now the warrior priest knew the creature recalled him as the one who had slipped the leash on that first day. It sent its coils up the wall, flailing just out of reach of him; anger and fear rose in it, as it saw one who was neither deceived nor threatened.

Recoiling, Zareft tore lengths of curtain and flung them down to hide the horror before searching among the tribute goods. His sword could perhaps have killed the thing he had seen nine years ago, but this grotesque magnification required drastic measures. It had grown a thousandfold, gorging on all brought before it, and he could guess that the stage was for hurling down its indiscriminate fare.

Among the stacks of tribute he found the rich oil of the olive groves of Lymnos, barrels of it, and a great cask of barley spirit. These would do the job. He rolled them forth, smashed them open with hammering blows of the sword and sent them over the edge, where they fell and splintered upon the gross body. Roars enough to wake the dead drowned out the guards' efforts. The alien knew its reign of black power was at an end. Zareft cast down a burning torch — turned and fled, as a wall of rushing steam engulfed the horror.

Its final cry shook the temple as if the stonework were struck with a mailed fist. Blocks fell from the roof, tore through the curtains and plummeted into the creature. It lashed the walls about it as the blazing lake of oil and spirit got hold, and its voice rose to a crescendo of fury and agony as Zareft rappelled the outside wall.

He abandoned his rope and turned, sword in hand, to meet the guards and entranced monks who threw themselves upon him. Many were the cries as his blade severed lance and shield, hacking home again and again to lay bodies on the flagstones as he recovered his ground toward the outer walls.

Smoke billowed in fetid palls from the windows and terraces. The earth shook as the Eminence writhed until, with the suddenness of a peal of thunder, the whole temple collapsed. It fell over the seawall as a rain of stone, pulverized tribute and blazing oil, and poured down the face of the mountain in a burning avalanche. Debris pummeled into the sea, an echo of the day when the star fell and set in play the whole cycle of events.

Silence followed the thunder. Zareft crouched, teeth bared, red sword in his hand, shoulders to the bare stone at his back and a circle of snarling faces all about him. But now the guards and monks seemed to wake — a tenacious hand released them as the last life went out of the Great God Sho'Tan in the cold waters below. Many dropped their weapons, staggering as if a puppet master had severed invisible cords which bound their bodies to its will.

In the clean flames was red redemption, and monks fell all about, their wasted bodies giving out as if only the power of the Eminence had animated them. They had starved a little at a time while it gorged, and now nothing was left to support them. Whatever vileness had gripped this temple was lifted away and the sea wind took the smoke up against the stars.

Zareft tapped swords aside with his blade and the guards stepped back, a great confusion in their faces. From over the roofs he heard a wailing — a pain in many hearts as memory returned of what had been; of the ways of right and wrong. With a slow stride he climbed to the high walls, up to the Tower of Retreat, and out onto its stone-flagged roof above which the highest banner flew. He sat cross-legged, sword across his knees, called down calm and meditated in silence while the sun came up before his eyes. The wind rustled his hair and gulls, startled by the commotion, drifted in the sky, white feathers rosy in the coming daylight.

It was a new day for the world. Zareft stood and raised his arms to the light, singing out, strong and loud, the invocation of the Sunhawk; and as he drew toward its close he heard a voice join in from below. With a smile on his lips he made his way down, all the way to the gates. He bade the guards open before him and strode down the mountain. A boy had run this path once, terrified of a new, dark god. A man now strode the way and the god was no more.

Messengers would ride to the king this day to bear witness that Sho'Tan was dead, and the stain of memory would fade as the Ram gave way to the Bull, and Bull to Twins. The Hawk and the Stag would return and the monastery on the Inland Sea would be rebuilt. Zareft would be there to make his world safe, but he was unsure what part he would play. He was a different person now, and bemused by the course of his loyalties — at the foot of the way he took a horse from the guard post by the pilgrim's camp, and turned to amble across the bridge into the rising sun.

He was going home to Freja.

Alien Rose
Guy Belleranti

They came,
they saw
and desired
what they saw,
huge pink alien roses.

So they raced from the spacecraft
shoving and tripping each other,
hoping to be first
to inhale the bouquet
of an alien rose.

But they found no sweet fragrance
upon burying their noses
in the pink petaled roses,
and instead found the flowers
had horrible odors.

Then, all of a sudden
the rose thorns became fangs,
and the petals turned red
as the greedy crew bled
until each one was dead.

The Dark
Randall Andrews

The scarlet light of the rising sun shone in smeary streaks through the towering buildings of the city center. At the crest of the Second Street Bridge, Joan Peters paused, turning her face into the warm rays as she caught her breath. Ten years earlier, she'd jogged over that bridge every day before going to work. Now here she was, rested and retired, and she couldn't walk over the damn thing without a break. Ten years was a long time.

The whole city seemed to have aged over the past decade, and not gracefully. From the comfort of her gated subdivision, it was easy for people like Joan to forget how many were struggling. It was incredible to think that less than a mile separated her fine home from a homeless shelter. Equally incredible was the fact that one of those shelter denizens had become her friend.

Joan spotted the younger woman a minute later, sitting at the top of the library stairs. She'd told Kim repeatedly that it wasn't necessary to wait for her, and she wouldn't bother telling her again. The truth was, the simple act of politeness was refreshing. None of the uppity old ladies from the country club would have waited—that was for damn sure.

"Morning, Kim," Joan called as she began the arduous climb.

"Good-good-good-morning," Kim replied, rising to her feet and stretching. She'd been sitting cross-legged, which was, oddly, the same way she sat in the library chairs. Kim was an astonishing collage of curiosities, including an array of ticks and twitches that matched her stutter, and a memory like a DVR. None of the young woman's eccentricities bothered Joan in the slightest. After a month of exploring old books together, she didn't even hear the stutter anymore.

As was their routine, the two women proceeded directly to the front desk, where they were greeted by the library's wizened director, Charles Wooden.

"Have I got a treat for you ladies today!" Charles said as they approached. "Four more boxes of donations showed up from Mrs. Garfield. Even at a glance, I can tell they're a treasure trove, just like the others."

In the year that Joan had been volunteering at the library, things had come a long way with her pet project, a local history section. Most of that progress was a result of her own hard work—and her money. The collection had received a boon the previous week from Martha Garfield, an elderly matriarch of one of the city's most prestigious families. Mrs. Garfield had decided ninety northern winters were enough, and was making a permanent move to West Palm Beach. The Pomeranian was going—the books were not.

Both women's faces lit up upon hearing of the new arrivals.

"Thank-thank-thank you, Mr. Wooden," Kim said, and then hurried away, obviously eager to see this new *treasure* for herself.

Joan caught the warm smile that blossomed on the old man's face and whispered, "I told you." He'd been reluctant when she'd suggested getting Kim involved in the project, but the young woman had won him over with her kind way and eagerness to help. Now they just needed to turn it into a paying job, something to help her get back on her feet. Hell, Joan would pay the wages herself if that's what it took. Kim was reluctant to accept charity, but that wouldn't be charity—not really. And besides, what she didn't know wouldn't hurt her.

By the time Joan caught up, Kim was already digging. A dozen volumes, mostly old hardcovers, were laid out across the room's ancient table, a massive slab of burnished oak. In her hands, she held another, smaller book. It was bound in cracked, black leather and sealed closed by a corroded, metal clasp.

"Oooh, that looks interesting," Joan said as she approached the table. "Is it locked shut, though?"

Unable to help herself, Kim picked gently at the clasp, and it immediately fell away, separating from the book and tumbling to the floor. Eyes flashing wide, she dropped the book on the table and jumped back, appearing ready to flee.

"It's okay, it's okay," Joan rushed to reassure her. "It was an accident. These books are old and fragile. We just need to be careful, alright?"

Tentatively, Kim nodded. She blew out a deep breath, and the panic faded from her face.

"Well, it's open now," Joan noted, "so we might as well have a look."

With care befitting a newborn, Joan lifted the book and began turning it over in her hands. She scrutinized the weathered cover, searching for some faded script or illustration, but none was visible. When at last she dared to separate the brittle, yellowed pages, she found them filled with intricate handwritten lines. The letters were sharp and severe, as if their author had scratched them down in a state of feverish haste. They slanted steeply to the left, making Joan wonder if they might have been written from right to left instead of what was, to her, the normal way. It hardly mattered. She had no idea what language they were written in, let alone what they said.

As she worked her way patiently through the pages, Joan became gradually aware that there was a symmetry to much of the text. Most of the lines were of similar length and were arranged into even numbered groups. Was this, she wondered, not a diary as she'd first suspected, but a book of poems?

Flipping the final page, her suspicion was confirmed. Penned across the inside of the back cover in plain English was a pair of simple, rhymed lines:

Let all the light within these walls,
Be snuffed from life as darkness falls.

With the tip of her index finger, Joan gently traced the lines as she read them silently to herself. As she did so, a cold chill crept inexplicably down the back of her neck. She wasn't a superstitious person, and the childish couplet, like something from a nursery rhyme, seemed hardly malevolent. And yet . . . the strange sense of foreboding lingered, refusing to fade.

From over her shoulder came Kim's whispering voice. As the young woman read the lines aloud, Joan's unease spiked, shocking her with a jolt of irrational fear. Her deepest, most primal instincts cried out, demanding action, but she remained still, frozen.

As if touched by a divine hand, Kim spoke the words slowly and clearly, without a single stutter. Only once did she err, substituting the word *without* where it should have been *within*.

"—*without these walls,*
—*as darkness falls.*"

The breath Joan had been holding remained lodged in her chest for several more seconds after Kim finished. When it finally broke free, it did so in a loud gasp that startled Kim as well.

"Are-are you okay?" she asked.

Joan blew out another deep breath and said, "Yes, I'm . . . fine. I just . . . I don't know. I had a weird feeling. But I'm fine."

Kim seemed not to have heard. Her head was suddenly tipped to the side, and her expression had become distant, as if she were straining to hear some faint sound. "It's so-so quiet," she whispered.

"Well, it is a library," Joan pointed out. "It's supposed to be—"

"Not-not-not in here," Kim interrupted. *"Out there."*

At first Joan didn't understand, but then it slowly dawned on her. Yes, it was always quiet in the library, but just beyond those walls lay city streets that bustled with activity day and night. Yet at that moment, she could hear none of it. She held her breath again, listening as closely as she could, but beneath the buzz of the fluorescent lights and the hum of the ventilation system, silence had descended. Had traffic been stopped? Had the streets been cleared? And the sidewalks, too? It was hard to imagine.

Very slowly, as if afraid to break the silence herself, Joan rose from her chair and crept back across the room. Every creak from the old hardwood floor seemed amplified and dangerous. Her own hurried breathing sounded obtrusive in the stillness.

As she stepped into the hallway, Joan had the strange thought that the light seemed different, too. A bit dimmer, perhaps? She hadn't noticed it before, but their workroom was windowless, lit only by the dingy fluorescence. The hallway, on the other hand, was typically flooded with natural light from the lobby, especially in the morning. But not now.

Three more creaking steps brought her within view of the front desk, where Charles was no longer seated, but standing, facing the library's entrance.

"What the hell?" Joan heard him mumble.

She thought he looked more confused than frightened, but that didn't stop her own fear from surging. Whatever he was looking at, it was going to be proof that her imagination wasn't playing tricks on her. What she was feeling was the result of something real. Something terrible.

Creeping forward to stand at Charles's side, Joan followed the man's gaze to the glass door, beyond which she saw . . . nothing. The outside world was gone, and in its place was depthless darkness. The book, which she'd absentmindedly carried with her, fell to the floor.

"What am I looking at?" Charles asked, still mumbling. Then pointing to a blackened window, he added, "And see there, it's not just the door. Is it . . .? Do you think . . .? What—the—*hell?*"

"Was-was-was it me?" Kim asked, making Joan jump. She hadn't heard the young woman follow her.

Joan took her by the shoulders, looked her square in the eyes, and said, "No. It wasn't you. That's not possible."

Even as she spoke the words, however, Joan doubted their validity. What Kim was suggesting, that she'd actually cast a spell or something, was ludicrous. She couldn't believe that. And yet, staring at that window, listening to the oppressive silence, she didn't know what to believe.

"It's not just dark like night, is it?" Charles asked as he started cautiously toward the door. "I mean, like if it was an eclipse or something. Even on the darkest night, that street stays lit like a carnival. There are stop lights, street lights, neon signs. And the power's not out, obviously."

"Even if it was," Joan interjected, "we'd have to be having an outage and an eclipse at the same time."

"I know, I know," Charles agreed. "He was nearly to the door now, leaning forward, squinting, lifting his glasses and then setting them back in place. "Has someone draped something across the glass, a tarp or blanket? And . . . the window, too, I guess? Except it's not just the dark, is it? It's *sooo* quiet out there. How can that be?"

The three of them stood there as the seconds slipped by, barely breathing, listening for any whisper of distant sound, staring at the impenetrable blackness on the other side of the glass.

The silence was eventually broken by a soft whimper. Joan turned to see Kim hugging herself and rocking back and forth in a frantic rhythm. She looked like a rabbit with nowhere to run and the scent of a wolf on the wind.

Before Charles could ask, Joan explained, "She read a little rhyme from one of those old books. She thinks that's what caused . . . whatever this is. But that's just silly. There's no such thing as a magic spell."

Again, Joan tasted the lie in the words as they crossed her tongue. The primitive part of her brain was practically screaming inside her. Despite what she'd *known* her whole life, the past five minutes had just slapped her in the face with a shocking new reality. Magic, or something akin to what she thought of as magic, had to be real. There was the proof, right in front of her nose.

"That's quite right, my dear," Charles said reassuringly. "I don't know what's happening here, but it's certainly not your fault. And it's certainly not magic. Now, enough wild conjecture. Let's try and find a real answer, shall we? Maybe we could hear something if we opened the door just a—"

"No!"

The word exploded from Joan like a shot fired accidentally by a hair trigger. Charles jerked his hand back from the door handle as Kim's whimpers turned to sobs.

"Joan, I'm surprised at you," Charles admonished, straightening his glasses. "You're a grown woman, an educated woman, and we have no reason to think we're in any danger. All we know is that it's dark out there. Surely, you're not afraid of the dark?"

"It's not that," Joan said, hating the quiver in her voice. "It's just . . . I just . . . I don't know."

"Oh, for goodness' sake," Charles huffed as he turned back to the door. As he slid his fingers around the handle,

Joan's heart raced. Behind her, Kim mumbled words of self-reproach as she continued to cry. Despite his outward confidence, Charles hesitated before pulling back the door. Just audibly, he whispered in echo, "For goodness' sake."

The door swung slowly inward, its hinges groaning in a way Joan had never noticed before. To her relief, the darkness did not flood in across the threshold, but remained still and silent and *outside*.

Turning his head to the side, Charles brought one ear slowly closer to the impossible barrier between the library's light and the blackness beyond. Only inches away, he stopped and closed his eyes, knitting his brows in concentration.

Never in her sixty-five years had Joan's pulse pounded as hard. She was queasy and lightheaded, swaying on her feet. Charles was so close—too close. She wanted—no, she *needed*—him to move back.

And then he did. He straightened himself as he turned to face the women, saying, "I can't hear a damn thing except Kim crying her head off. I'm sorry, my dear, but could you please—"

The pale gray arms that snatched the old man away moved so quickly, they seemed to defy nature. As Kim ran screaming through the library, Joan stood petrified, starring at the empty space where her friend had stood. Her mind seized like an overheated engine. The image of those lightning limbs flashed before her eyes—the hairless forearms, the outstretched fingers, the ashen skin, like something that died at sea and then rode the tides for days before finally washing ashore.

When she returned to her senses, Joan found herself shuffling backward. Summoning her last reserve of adrenaline-induced courage, she reversed course, charging forward, throwing herself against the door, slamming it shut. Her eyes filled with tears as her nose crunched against the glass. As she staggered, struggling to keep her feet beneath her, she noticed the small smear of crimson she'd left behind. With the terrible black behind it, the blood was barely visible until the pale fingertip reached to it from the other side.

"No. No-no-no. No-no-no-no-no."

Joan was backpedaling again, but her eyes remained fixed on the nightmare at the door. When she stepped on the abandoned book, she lost her balance and fell hard on her tailbone. The book flipped open, settling with seeming intent so that the translated spell was facing her—*taunting* her.

The refrain of Joan's denial cut off abruptly with the impact, and in its place the dread silence returned. Except . . . not quite.

Barely able to think, Joan vaguely realized the quiet was not absolute. She could hear a faint voice in the distance, Kim's voice. It took a moment to realize what she was saying.

"Kim, no!" Joan tried to shout, but her words only squeaked out, barely taking flight before being absorbed by the books and the buzz of the fluorescent bulbs. She tried again, but the result was the same. "Kim, no. Why?"

Even as she asked the question, the answer came to her. What was it Kim had said earlier? *It's my fault. I read it wrong.* So now she thought she could undo her mistake by reciting it again—correctly? Which, with her memory, she could. Where was her mistake again?

Without. *Within.*

"Kim, no."

When the lights went out, Joan's mind fled to a distant memory, when the kids were still young and they'd taken a family camping trip to the Dakotas. She'd grudgingly acquiesced to a cave tour despite her dislike of tight spaces and her secret fear of the dark. She'd managed to soldier through it until their guide killed the lights, offering a moment of true darkness, something rarely experienced on the surface. The result had been the worst panic attack of Joan's life.

It was one of her most toxic memories, yet she clung to it with the desperation of someone drowning, grabbing at anything that might keep her afloat. Those long dark seconds in the cave had traumatized her, but she'd made it out. She'd survived. More than that, they'd sat around a fire that night, eating s'mores and arguing over which presidents they'd see the next day in the stone.

That was where she hid. The memory became a bunker in her brain, her psychic panic room. So completely did she immerse herself into that page from her past, she could actually smell the smoke from the fire, feel its warmth against her legs. Her senses flooded with details from the scene she wouldn't have dreamed she could recall. The memory enveloped her utterly, occupying every corner of her consciousness, leaving none of her mental machinery available for anything else, including perception. Which was a blessing.

She didn't even feel the touch of the cold hands when they found her there in the dark.

Tanka

fall of Earth
controlled numbers
human mating season
alien reproduction permit
rose-scented sheets

~Tyree Campbell

The Happy Harper Home
Glen R. Stripling

When Bob Harper walked in the front door of his house, his heart leapt with great joy for finally being home. For quite some time he felt that way every evening. To him coming home made him feel like a child at Disney World or a teenager on his first date.

He walked into his office and smiled as he saw Glenda, his home receptionist. She was seated at her small desk scanning her screen with a calculating look as she typed in data into the word processor.

"Hello, Glenda."

She turned to him slightly and gave him an appropriate smile. "Good evening, Sir," she answered as she continued typing.

"Did I get any calls?" he asked.

"You got one seven minutes and twenty-six seconds ago from Utopia. Mr. Harris said they have some questions about the software they are designing for you."

"They could have asked me before I left the factory but that's OK."

"I made some calls myself about your dishwasher. Your repairman is at home with the flu. So I got on the net and searched for repairmen in this area. I found one named Lacey Carter and told her the problem. She says you may have a bad sensor and she will be here at 8:30 in the morning and take a look at it."

"Great! Well Glenda, do you know what today is?"

"April the twenty-sixth Sir."

"And you know what that is?" She turned to him. "This is National Secretaries Day! You are my secretary, so I bought you this." And he gave her a small white box. She took the box, deftly opened it and found a small bottle with an atomizer. She sprayed some on her fingers and gasped slightly, as she smelled the aroma.

"Channel No. 5?"
"You like it?"
"Yes...if it's alright with your wife."

"It is, Glenda. Marsha is not the least bit jealous of you. She and Marie love you just as much as I do. You are part of us. You make us happy." He gently kissed her forehead. Then he noticed a wonderful smell.
"What's that I smell?"
"It's a surprise for you, Sir. I've been instructed not to say." He traced the smell to Maria's bedroom and grinned.
"You don't have to. I already know what it is." She turned to him and gave him a slight Mona Lisa smile.
He strolled through the house until he saw Martha setting the table for him in the dining room.
"Hey, Bob!" she crooned. "You're just in time. I got a great supper for you."
"I think you do," he said as he was slightly stunned by the wondrous aroma drifting from the kitchen. "What's that I smell?" He gently kissed her chilly cheek.
She gently embraced his waist with her right arm. "T-bone steak," she answered. "I also have potatoes baking in the oven. And we got broccoli on the stove with melted cheese. I know you like it that way."
"What is the occasion?" asked Bob. "What are we celebrating?"
"We are celebrating," she said sweetly, "the fact you are home for the day!" She gave him a gentle kiss. "By the way," she added, "Maria is working on a surprise for you."
"Oh?"
"Daddy!" He turned to see the child walking briskly. She was almost running and somehow managing not to spill the food she was carrying on a large saucer. "I got a surprise for you!"
"Really! What is it Honey?"
"Well remember the EZ-Bake oven you got me for my birthday?"
"Yeah?"
"Well today I used it to make your dessert tonight. I made you these brownies!"

"Oh my goodness! I was wondering what that wonderful smell was!" He took the saucer, placed it on the dining room table and reached to embrace her. "Oh Honey thank you! Give Daddy a hug." He was just barely able to barely able to lift her eighty-pound body off the floor and kissed her forehead. Like her mother's, the child's skin was a bit cool to the touch but the experience meant the world to him. "I can't wait to try one." And he could not.

"Mommy says we have to wait until after dinner before we eat dessert."

He smiled. "Alright. Fair enough."

"You two sit down while I finish cooking," instructed Marsha. Bob and Marie sat down and they smiled at each other.

"So what all can you cook in your EZ Bake?" asked Bob.

"Oh I can cook lots of things!" claimed the delighted child. "I can cook brownies, chocolate chip cookies, sugar cookies, peanut butter cookies, cakes…a whole lot of things!"

"Goodness gracious! You are turning into a little chef!" Bob answered with glee. "We need to get you to help Moma cook."

"Daddy?" Bob looked at her. "What do you do at work?"

"Well…I do a lot of things. I'm the president."

"Like George Washington?" Bob smiled again.

"No. I'm not the president of America. I am a company president. I am the president of Utopia."

"What's Utopia?"

"Utopia is a place where everybody is happy. Like we are. We make things that make people happy."

"What kind of things?"

"I tell you what, Honey," Bob began with a warm smile. "Tomorrow you, me, Moma and Miss Glenda will all go to Daddy's work together. You will get to see everything we do. I promise you will see it all."

"That will be fun!" And the child's face lit up.

*****

"This is the first time I had to upgrade the AI software of three bots in one night," said Hubert Stanford, the Chief Engineer of Utopia Enterprises.

"What's going on?" asked his co-worker Margaret.

"Harper is bringing his family droids here in the morning. We'll have to download the updated software and implant heaters under the skins to simulate human body temperature. I hope it makes him happy."

It Wasn't Silly Putty
Terrie Leigh Relf

Late last night, a cargo box was abandoned on the off-ramp to a local park. A packing statement found at the scene was labeled as children's toys, but none of the merchandise was located. Torn packaging of indeterminate origin was also located in trash bins at the nearby park, along with a pink gooey residue. Since no one has come forward to claim ownership, investigators are perplexed as to what occurred and who might be to blame.

    taking imprints
    of our children
    alien archeologist

For more where this came from, try "Postcards from Space." Here's the ordering link:
https://www.hiraethsffh.com/product-page/postcards-from-space-by-terrie-leigh-relf

Nuclear Insect
Denny Marshall

Becoming Jade by Tyree Campbell
Reviewed by Lisa Timpf

In *Becoming Jade,* Tyree Campbell takes the reader on an adventure that is part mystery, part internal journey, and part exploration of a new and bizarrely different world. We learn several things early in the story as protagonist Annae approaches, then lands on, the planet Deege. Annae is a killer-for-hire, or a mortifice. She has been hired by Pekon Magness, Director of Projects for Corporatia Construction and Maintenance, to complete a mission. Annae, unbeknownst to Magness, has an end game of her own.

Deege, the planet Annae visits to perform the assignment, is inhabited by druzies, entities that are described thus: "Humanoid in appearance, the garbless druzy came in a variety of pastel skin colors, aqua and turquoise the most common, with caps of black head hair and otherwise hairless bodies." The druzies carry around plants called moodmartins, and Magness has told Annae he believes there is some kind of symbiotic relationship between the two.

The assignment as laid out by Magness, is simple: Annae has to kill a moodmartin and capture a druzy. Annae doesn't know what Magness wants with the druzy, but if she has her way, he won't live long enough to enact his plans once the delivery has been made. Annae hopes that obtaining the druzy will enable her to get close enough to Magness to kill him, in reprisal for the role he had in the death of Annae's beloved twin sister, Ming.

Though Annae is initially confident the mission will be a quick one, she encounters unexpected obstacles. One of the biggest setbacks is the loss of her comm device, which is tossed into the swamp by a druzy. The comm device represents Annae's only way of communicating with, and entering, her space vessel. Until she finds a way to get back in, there's no point completing the assignment, so Annae decides to focus on finding out more about druzies, moodmartins, and what's really going on here on Deege.

As events unfold, the reader gets glimpses into Annae's past, including happier times spent with Ming. Annae's mental conversations with Ming illuminate the closeness of the bond the two had when Ming was alive, and illustrate Annae's difficulties letting go of the sense of pain, loss, and guilt that accompanied her sister's death. Meanwhile, in the here-and-now, Annae has her hands full trying to figure out how she's going to complete her assignment.

Deege's geography, flora, and fauna are described in sufficient detail to render them real for the reader. Deege is a different world, though not so different as to make it impossible to imagine:

> The lower trail wound through stands of waist-high reeds and vanished in the spongy premarsh. Root-bound mud threatened to devour Annae's boots, and she retreated to solid ground, surveying the marsh. It filled a depression between the glen and a long low rise a hundred meters to the south. Beyond the crest of that rise Annae, squinting against the sunlight that glistened off the water between the reed clumps, could make out the spare upper canopy of a low forest. Before her, stalks of pink flowers that rose from head-sized, floating green nodules troped toward the northeast . . .

The terms for Annae's vessel, her weaponry, and her accessories (such as glowstones, which capture heat from the sun and radiate it back out at night) add to the sense of difference.

In addition to scene-setting, Campbell's descriptions evoke emotion:

> Dusk faded past indigo, and the glowstones cast much of the glen in a spectral tangerine. All along the tree line gnarled shadows queued up, poised to exploit latent fears. Analogs of insects and birds began a fitful cacophony comprehensible only to themselves, a vibrant overture for the rest of the night. Annae shivered in anticipation. How much longer before the druzies came out to play? And what of nocturnal predators?

Becoming Jade incorporates subtle humor as well. On one occasion, Annae reflects on her assignment: "She had only to snap the moodmartin in half like a twig. Well, it *was* a twig." On another, she notes that "Circumstances had conspired against her, and were winning."

Suspense is maintained through the story, as Annae herself faces a series of baffling encounters, making life on Deege a puzzle she needs to solve in order to survive.

There are sufficient twists and turns along the way to keep things interesting, including Annae's discovery that Magness didn't know as much as he thought he did about the relationship between druzies and moodmartins. If you'd like to find out the real story, check out *Becoming Jade*.

To order a copy of Becoming Jade, go here: https://www.hiraethsffh.com/product-page/becoming-jade-by-tyree-campbell

Beautiful Death
Sandy DeLuca

The Healer's Apprentice
Jason Lairamore

The morning was damp. Heavy gray clouds pressed upon the lonely hill where Master Brock's Miraculous Apothecary shop sat. Anric Harmod, Master Brock's new apprentice, cleaned the front room just as he had been instructed before his Master's leaving earlier that morning.

"Anric Harmod is wearing the blue stripe of a healer. What a sight," came a voice from behind.

Mr. Jiles Morely stood in the doorway wearing an open grin on his dirt-smeared face. He was a neighbor who shared fields with Anric's father. They were of the legendary foothill farmers whose produce was the greatest in the world. Their fruits and vegetables possessed the very essence of life itself thanks to the magical waters that descended from Lifebringer Mountain.

That Anric had left such a highly lucrative and highly respected life in order to be a lowly apprentice had caused many, including his own father, to question his good sense. Mr. Morely was one of the few exceptions.

"What brings you here, Mr. Morely? Master Brock is away minding his garden." To the north lay a rolling wood where Master Brock raised his various herbs.

Mr. Morely shook his head. The muscles on his neck were thick cords that writhed like snakes when he moved. "I was leaving Sadietown from selling a bit of early cabbage when I thought I'd stop by to see how you fared." His smile was wide, showing many strong, pearly-white teeth.

"My first week has gone well so far," Anric replied.

Mr. Morely came fully into the shop and set one of his great hands on Anric's shoulder. "I'm proud of you Anric. It takes a lot for a boy to become a man, and it takes more if that boy decides to grow out from under his family's shadow."

"Yes, sir," Anric replied.

"Make your dreams come true, you hear?"

"I will." He planned on doing just that. His dreams just weren't what anybody else thought.

Mr. Morely nodded and turned to go. Anric couldn't help but notice that he was limping.

"Mr. Morely, what happened to your leg?" It wasn't like Mr. Morely to ever be hurt.

"What, you looking for your first patient?" he asked.

Anric shook his head.

"It'd be an honor," Mr. Morely continued.

"I can't Mr. Morely. Master Brock's locked up the apothecary."

Mr Morely sat right there on the floor of the front room and pulled up his pants leg. On his shin was a closed slice. It was so thin that Anric could barely see it.

"What happened there?" he asked.

"You've a good eye," Mr. Morely said. "No even my wife could see that cut. It happened this morning while I was at harvest for the cabbage."

Anric poked on it. The wound didn't look angry. There were no signs of infection. It was a little warm, but that was just the body adding some circulation to the area to promote healing.

"What happened?"

"Funny thing. I don't recall other than it happened in the field this morning. Doesn't even hurt."

'So why was he limping?' Anric thought. Something didn't add up. The wound was too thin, too perfect. He went to lay his hands on it again to do some deeper palpation when a deep voice caused him to jump.

"Do not touch him," the voice said.

A dwarf, wearing various blades and cinched sacks on his person, came toward them with quick, purposeful strides. Anric was struck dumb. He'd not seen many dwarves in his fifteen years, and to have one enter the shop so suddenly, and with such measured concentration, was almost enough to turn him to stone.

"Get back, boy. Where is your master?" the dwarf asked.

"Away, tending his stock," he managed to say as he scooted away.

Before Mr. Morely even had a chance to utter a word, the dwarf was upon him. He knocked Mr. Morely back then sat on his stomach, his face toward Mr. Morely's feet.

"What are you doing?" Mr. Morely asked through clenched teeth. It was a wonder he could talk at all. Dwarves were heavy. Their bones were of iron and their muscles of granite.

The dwarf raised a couple of bushy eyebrows. He pulled out a paring knife from one of his breast pockets and a hatchet from a hoop at his hip.

"I'll give you a choice," he said. "I don't usually give a choice."

He turned his head and smiled down at Mr. Morely. The dwarf's teeth were silver. "You want to keep your leg or not?"

Mr. Morely tried to throw the dwarf from him, but it was no use.

"Help me, Anric. This dwarf's gone mad."

But Anric was frozen stiff. He'd never been in a fight in his life. His heart raced at the mere possibility.

The Dwarf shrugged. "Have it your way," he hefted the ax and readied to swing.

"Keep the leg! Keep the leg!" Mr. Morely screamed.

"Are you sure? Amputation is less painful, believe me."

Mr. Morely nodded. His face was pale, his eyes wide. The dwarf replaced the ax and felt around the wound with his free hand.

"This just might work," he said and looked up to Anric. "Boy, get his feet. Help me keep him on the floor. He's not going to like this."

"What are you going to do?" Mr. Morely asked. The trembling fear in Mr. Morely's voice disturbed Anric more than anything.

The dwarf put the blade between his teeth and leaned forward. He placed one grimy thumb on either side of the wound, and wrapped the rest of his meaty hands around Mr. Morely's calf. Anric took Mr. Morely's ankles and pushed them to the floor.

With a grunt, the dwarf ripped open the slit in Mr. Morely's shin. Mr. Morely screamed so loud the timbers of the shop shook. He grabbed at the dwarf and hit him in the back over and over, to no avail.

Anric barely hung on to Mr. Morely's ankles. The wound, when opened, exploded out in vile green putrescence that splattered all over his new apprentice robes. The smell was so awful he could taste it all the way to the bottom of his stomach.

The dwarf held the wound open with one slimy green hand and took his knife in the other. In quick succession he sliced great grey-green hunks from Mr. Morely's leg. Mr. Morely slammed his fist to the floor hard enough to crack the hardwood.

"Ahah!" the dwarf yelled, and pulled out a yellowish ball the size of Anric's thumb from the wound. "The seed," he said.

Mr. Morely was no longer fighting. He lay there sweating and gasping for air. The dwarf stood and eyed the yellow ball for a moment. Then he dropped it to the floor and squished it under his boot.

"You'll be fine," he said. "Lucky for you I was here. In a few hours you'd have fully turned."

"What was that?" Mr. Morely asked.

The dwarf ignored him and shook his head. "When'd you get that wound?" he asked.

Mr. Morely told the dwarf what Anric already knew.

All the blood drained away from the dwarf's face as he listened to the tale. "You're a foothill farmer, a real foothill farmer?" he asked.

"What's left of me," Mr. Morely said.

The dwarf's eyes lost their focus.

"It's made it to Lifebringer," he said in a hush.

The haunted words were just out of his mouth when a scream rent the air. Anric knew that voice. He could have identified it from anywhere.

The owner of that voice was the reason he'd left his family fortune and entered apprenticeship. She was the dream that he wanted to come true, though she did not yet know it.

He was out of the door and headed toward the sound before he'd even known he'd moved. He saw her right away once he'd made it outside. It was as if his eyes knew instinctively where to look.

Lysa Kairis was on her knees in front of a great shaggy horse that must have belonged to the dwarf. She had her face in her hands and she was crying. His heart ached so hard it made his neck hurt.

But it wasn't the crying that was truly bothersome. Lysa was covered in blood and her clothes were in tatters.

He ran to her and took her in his arms. He'd always wanted to do that, just not like this.

"Lysa, what happened?" He felt like a helpless fool. Here lay the girl of his dreams, hurt, and he didn't know what to do about it.

Lysa didn't answer, such were her wracking sobs. He gently pulled her hands away from her face in an effort to see into her eyes, to make sure she was whole.

She wasn't whole. Great gashes crossed her face. Her flesh hung open to show exposed bone. Her bottom lip was cut to the jaw. More than a few of her teeth were missing. The end of her nose was not there. Her once beautiful blonde tresses sat askew on the top of her head. A gentle pressure showed where her scalp had been partially cut back. A red line ran along the top of her forehead as evidence of the deep cut.

Miraculously, none of these wounds seemed to be bleeding.

"Do you know this wood fairy, boy?" the dwarf asked from behind him.

He nodded, unable to speak. Lysa's eyes were empty. She looked so lost.

"I happened upon a giant gnole in the process of destroying a thatch hut at the edge of the wood north of here. The girl took a glancing blow from the thing's claws. I was able to dispatch the monster and dress her wounds. She was muttering something about a healer. I saw the shop and came seeking help."

"Her mother? Her father?" Mr. Morely asked. He must have regained his feet and somehow made it outside. Tough man, Mr. Morely was.

"Nothing remained," the dwarf answered. "I burnt the creature with the house."

Anric couldn't stop shaking his head. He couldn't stop staring at the once beautiful face of Lysa. She looked devastated. She looked destroyed. He had to do something for her, anything.

He let her go and ran back into the shop. He tried forcing the lock of the apothecary then he tried using his shoulder. There were medicines in there, magical salves that could restore Lysa. He just knew it. There had to be. Master Brock was a famous master, known across the land.

"Help me", he called when he couldn't find a way to get inside. He turned imploringly toward the dwarf. If anybody could get inside, he could.

But the dwarf shook his head. "I'll not do it," he said. "Only by the master's leave can one enter his shop."

He ran back outside. Mr. Morely was on his wagon. His face was pale.

"Come, Anric. Gather up Lysa and we will go to your father. She will be safe there."

Anric shook his head. He'd not left his family only to go running back when times got dangerous. Besides, Lysa needed Master Brock's help, not his father's.

"Thank you, Mr. Morely, but no. I must seek out my master."

Mr. Morely looked pained at Anric's decision, but Anric could not help it.

"Are there others in your household," The dwarf asked Mr. Morely.

"My wife"

"It would be a good idea to check her for wounds such as yours," The dwarf said.

The possibility that his wife might actually be in danger flashed across Mr. Morely's broad features in a shockwave.

"Yes, I must be away," he said. "Take an extra care, Anric." He started his wagon down the hillock without waiting for Anric's reply.

Anric turned to the dwarf. There was his 'extra care', if he could get it.

"Will you help me find my master?" he asked.

The dwarf nodded. "Your master needs to know what lies before us. His healing arts will be invaluable."

Anric was also thinking of Master Brock's healing arts. He needed to get Lysa the help she needed. It was the only thing he could think to do.

* * *

Anric's horse wasn't the obvious war horse the dwarf's animal was. His was a broad back plow animal that was all strength and stamina, but no speed. As much as he'd have liked to have galloped the whole way into the rolling northern wood, he was stuck at a steady walk. Lysa, her sobs subsided, clung silently to his back as they made their slow way.

"What's going on, Mr. Dwarf?" he asked. There'd never before been monsters here. Monsters were things talked about. They didn't exist, not in his world.

The dwarf cleared his throat. "Call me Brinol, boy."

"Yes sir," he said, and waited for Brinol to continue.

They rode in silence for a moment.

"A monster maker got through our northeastern border," Brinol finally said.

Such things were supposed to be impossible. The borders possessed layer after layer of protective spell. Nothing could cross without the proper due process.

Brinol looked away and toward the approaching north wood where they hoped to soon find Master Brock. They'd purposely taken the path farthest from Lysa's home so as to not upset her further, if such was possible.

"I was close to where the border was hit, so I thought I'd go see what manner of creature had stumbled and died on our doorstep. I never expected to see a maker. Makers don't come near the border. They know better."

"It somehow survived the spells?" Anric asked.

The dwarf shook his head. "No. It was dead. It was more than dead."

"More than dead?" he asked, but the dwarf wasn't listening.

"The guards arrived. None of us had ever seen a maker hit the border spells before."

"What do the makers look like?"

"Makers look like men, almost exactly like men, except for their eyes and the sound of their voices. But fear not, you would never misplace one for a man, not ever, even if it ever let you see it. They are good at hiding."

"But the maker at the border was dead?" Anric asked.

"Yes, it was dead. Its stomach was wide open, like it'd exploded as it'd run through the border spells. Its entrails were lying close by, strewn behind it like a tangled up mess of vines."

Anric shook his head then it came to him.

"The maker sacrificed itself to sneak another in," he said.

Brinol showed him his silver teeth. "Leave it to an unlearned boy to nail the answer on its head. That's the way of it, alright. Of course, none of the guards seemed to agree with that conclusion, seeing as how makers don't act like that, not ever in the history of the land."

"So," Anric knit his brows. "You've come alone? Help is not on the way?

Brinol nodded. "As of now, that's how it sits. The giant gnole at the cabin was the first proof I was right. The foothill farmer's wound confirmed my worst fears."

He tried hard not to tremble as the reality of it all hardened around him, but his hands did shake. Lysa, still quiet, moved her arms from his waist and took one of his hands in hers. It was the first sign of actual life he'd seen from her since he'd found her screaming by the shop. It felt good to hold her hand.

* * *

They reached the edge of the wood and stopped. Brinol dismounted and eyed the deceptively friendly trees.

"There are two types of people in this world, boy," The dwarf said offhandedly as he scanned the trees. "You're either the feared, or the fearful." He turned his bushy head toward Anric. "The fearful may survive, but they don't ever solve the problem at hand. And we got ourselves one big problem."

Anric nodded, but felt like he didn't truly know the depth of Brinol's words. All this was too big. He kept his intensity directed toward something he understood. Lysa. He'd find a way to restore her. That was all that mattered.

Brinol turned back to the wood and rubbed at his chin. "I've been through my share of wood," he said. "This one feels like it's trying to hide something."

Anric turned to look at Lysa, her head was down. She slid from his plow horse and walked to the wood.

Anric dismounted as well.

"Why isn't she talking?" he asked Brinol quietly when he reached the dwarf's side. Lysa walked on, so they followed her into the gentle shade under the trees.

"You ever tried to talk with your face half cut off?" Brinol asked. "It's painful."

Anric's heart ached even more.

"She will take us to Master Brock's secret garden," he said. "She and her family are the only ones that know how to get there."

Brinol nodded, his eyes darting everywhere. "Slow down, lass. Let me keep a sharp eye on things. Monsters may be about."

And one was about, though it wasn't Brinol who saw it first. Anric caught a twitch out of the corner of his eye. Something had moved. He knew it, but he could see nothing when he looked.

Some deeper sense kept him quiet as he took a jump toward Lysa. He grabbed her and yanked her away just as something leaped at them. It was too big for his mind to grasp. He could not fathom how the thing had been hiding at all. All he could do was shake his head and try not to freeze up as the awesome thing advanced.

Brinol gave a great yell and the monster curled up upon itself in shock. It was afraid.

"Come, boy," Brinol called. "Don't be afraid of a spider." He danced in and sliced off one of the creatures legs.

"This one is a baby yet." The spider writhed at the loss of limb, but Brinol did not finish it. The dwarf instead grabbed a hold of Anric's arm and placed in his hand the weapon he'd used to injury the beast.

"A good falchion is a lot like an ax. Chop it, boy. Show it you're not afraid."

The sword felt heavy in his hand, though he knew it to be much less than the maul he'd used to split wood back home. He didn't have much time to ponder on it though, because the spider, a giant creature the size of a cow, was once again coming at them. He glanced to Lysa, but it was hard to tell what she was thinking with her face as messed up as it was. And, the dwarf only smiled at him, as if nothing out of the ordinary was going on.

He brandished the weapon and yelled. The spider reared at him, showing fangs longer than his hands. He danced around to see what the spider would do, but it only shifted its aggressive pose to stay in front of him.

"What do I do?" he called, still slicing the air, still dancing.

"Do what you do to any spider. Squish it," Brinol said at his back with a laugh.

Anric had no idea how to go about doing that, not with the thing reared up and ready. He decided to try to take out one of the thing's legs, just as the dwarf had done. Brinol had made it look easy enough.

He danced around and tried to judge the spider's speed. When he thought he had it down, he made his move.

But the spider moved faster. It jumped as he jumped and was on top of him before he knew what'd happened. All of a sudden he was grappling with the thing's thorax, trying to keep those wicked looking fangs away from him.

And still, the dwarf laughed.

Then the spider stopped its thrashing and jumped away. He was on his feet just as fast, wondering what had happened and looking for the sword he'd dropped at the same time.

He found the sword and heard Lysa's scream. She was on the spiders back and it was trying to buck her off.

He took a step toward the action. In the time it took him to move that one foot forward the spider had freed itself of Lysa. It pinned her down on the ground and sank its fangs into her shoulder.

The dwarf ripped the falchion from his hands, stepped to the spider, and cut the creature in half. He kicked it away from Lysa and squished it by jumping on its head and thorax with both feet.

He pulled out one of his cinched bags and sprinkled powder over Lysa's wound. After that he pulled a corked bottle from the inside of his overshirt and had her take a good pull of its contents.

Brinol had done all this in the time it took Anric to rush up to where Lysa lay on the ground.

"That little fairy's got more gumption than you, boy," Brinol said. Anric looked to Lysa then back to Brinol, who was repositioning his supplies.

"From the looks of things I thought you cared for her," he said. "I must have read that wrong."

The words devastated Anric. He looked down upon Lysa, but could see nothing but pain there. He'd done nothing to help her. She'd acted to save him, and he'd not even had the time to help her. He had nothing to say to the dwarf, nothing that was worth a hill of beans. He'd failed Lysa, plain and simple.

After a few moments Lysa stood and continued. She never said a word, never complained. Anric knew she must have been hurting something awful.

*   *   *

They found Master Brock a while later. At first glance, he appeared to be resting against a rock. Anric thought all was well, and relaxed some. Master Brock would know what to do. He could help.

Then he saw the flickering sheen of a protective orb surrounding the master healer.

Brinol did a quick scan. "This place is clean," he said.

They walked closer to Master Brock's unstable orb.

Herbs of all kinds grew in little knots in every corner of the little undulation between the low hills. Every color and every smell Anric could imagine wafted on the gentle wind. It was so intoxicating he found himself looking everywhere and sniffing, all at once.

"This was a clean place." Master Brock's voice sounded crackly dry. The master saw Lysa and tried to raise an arm toward her, but failed halfway through.

"I'm so sorry, Little Lysa. So sorry"

"Explain," Brinol said. The dwarf looked nervous. He fidgeted from foot to foot and his eyes darted here and there.

"She found me unawares," Master Brock said. He better arranged his limbs within his blue robe of healing mastery. The effort it took was written on his face.

Brinol's rough, worn face went pale. "She? It can't be. There's not been a female maker since before King Roo first joined the civil races."

A tear rolled down Master Brock's wrinkled face as he nodded. "Her name is Mahain. She wants what we have."

Brinol fell to his knees before the orb. The entire wood seemed to fall silent.

Anric glanced to Lysa. Her broken face was rigid as she stared at Master Brock.

"What do we have that the monster wants?" Anric asked. Master Brock rolled his eyes toward him. The whites of the master's eyes were shot through with black. The bones of his face appeared to be writhing under the skin.

"Life, boy," Brinol answered. "We have Lifebringer Mountain. The monsters want it."

Master Brock groaned. His protective orb pulsed like an unsteady heartbeat. He opened his blue robe with trembling hands. His bony chest had three perfect slices that looked just like the one Mr. Morely had had on his shin.

"Master Dwarf, I have a need of you," Master Brock said hoarsely.

Brinol drew his falchion. "Aye"

Lysa's sobs followed the dwarf's words. Anric put a tentative arm around her shoulder and she collapsed against his chest, trembling.

"Wait," he called. Master Brock's eyes were twice their normal size. The white had almost completely turned to black. His mouth stretched nearly from ear to ear.

His magic was fading. He was turning into a monster.

"How do I help Lysa?" he asked the hungry face that'd once been Master Brock.

The orb held, but it was coming and going. Master Brock darted out a forked tongue in Anric's direction.

"Life blood from the maker," it hissed. "Given by a ..."

The orb collapsed with a pop. Brinol leaped forward with a yell and beheaded the still changing form of Master Brock.

Lysa sagged in Anric's arms. She'd passed out. He lowered her to the soft turf.

Brinol stood over what once had been Master Brock.

"You may want to turn away," he said. "I still have to find the seeds."

* * *

Brinol had to carry Lysa from the woods. Anric lacked the strength. The dwarf didn't even ask. He just picked her up and started back the way they'd come. Anric followed from a step behind.

"Brinol, can we take Lysa to my dad? She will be safe there." He needed to make sure she was alright before going out to do what he had in mind. He'd not wanted to involve his family in his business, but it looked like he had no choice.

"Where do they live?" Brinol asked quietly. The dwarf seemed distracted. His worry for their situation was evident in his bearing.

"My dad is a foothill farmer," he said.

Brinol glanced back at him, his question written on his scruffy face. He was wondering, as everyone did, what Anric was doing as a healer's apprentice when he'd been born into one of the prestigious lines of foothill farmers.

He loved Lysa, that was why, but he didn't say it.

"That's a fine plan, boy," Brinol said. "I can drop you off there as well, on my way."

Anric didn't respond. He just kept pace. Lysa would be safe with his family.

It didn't take long to exit the wood.

Their horses came at their whistles and soon they were on their way. They skirted the hill and continued around to join the paths leading toward civilization. Anric led them toward the foothills.

The morning progressed as they traveled in silence. The sun burnt away the clouds to give way to a pleasantly cool spring day. The change from a pressed-down gray sky to one of light-hearted blue was such a metamorphosis that it made it seem that the horrific activities of the morning were but a dream.

Then he'd see Lysa lying across Brinol's lap.

"Brinol, what was Master Brock turning into?" he asked.

Brinol clenched his jaw then shot him a quick glance. "I don't know, and it doesn't matter," he said. "The seeds take the host in the direction they want to go."

"So, that spider?" Anric asked.

"That was a deer or another animal. They shift fast and make big, powerful monsters, but they are as about as smart as their animal counterpart."

They rode for a few more moments in silence. The tension radiating from Brinol seemed to be getting worse.

"A female maker worries you," Anric said. It was obvious.

Brinol nodded. "The makers are immortal," he said. "And they are all male. They reproduce by granting their life power to their offspring. It doesn't happen very often. At least we don't think it does."

"So having a female means something extra?" Anric asked.

Brinol looked at him and held his eye. "The last female maker was Queen Krehain, ruler before King Roo joined us to fight."

"Krehain the Witch? But, that's only a story."

Anric's horse stopped its plodding and jerked at the reins just as a neighing shriek rent the air. They were in a shallow valley between two foothills. The shriek came again, from up ahead, only to be cut off mid-shriek.

The dwarf's horse had no such qualms about the horrific noises. Brinol trotted on up ahead, slow, drawing his falchion as he stood in the saddle.

Anric jumped from his stubborn mount and ran to catch up.

A black snake bigger around than he was and more than fifteen paces long had a horse in its mouth. It wrenched the recently dead horse's head one way then another.

Another snake, a twin of the first, circled a wagon. Its head bobbed up and down as it eyed the two people riding the wagon's seat.

It was his mom and dad.

Dad had one arm around Mom and the other up so that the snake might see it. They were both very still, except for moving to keep the snake in front of them.

"That's my parents," he told Brinol.

Brinol slid from his mount and set Lysa on the ground. He tossed the falchion to the turf at Anric's feet and pulled out a pair of throwing knives from a row he had wrapped around his chest.

"Go save your folks, if you can," he said and walked away toward the snake holding the horse.

Brinol was testing him again, he just knew. He was waiting for him to freeze, so that he could confirm that he was afraid. He looked to Lysa lying helpless on the ground. She twitched as if she'd soon come around.

He was afraid, he really was.

He picked up the falchion and ran straight toward the snake harassing his parents. The thing could strike at any time and his parents would be dead. He'd not be witness to that, not without a fight, scared or no.

"Hey!" he yelled. "Hey, leave them alone."

Both snakes jerked their head in his direction then both came at him.

He stopped running, his eyes widening. The black snakes kept their head low as they advanced.

He brandished his sword, and readied himself. He imagined roots growing through his feet. He didn't want to run away. He couldn't outrun the snakes anyway.

His muscles felt weak as water. The first of the snakes reached him and stopped no more than five feet from him. He swung his sword at it and it retreated back a little.

The second snake arrived. They lifted their heads, almost in unison, to a height well over his head.

His hands were slick on the falchion and his mouth was dry. He tried to tense, to get ready for the strike he knew was to come, but his muscles had seemed to have already given up. Keeping the sword up was a considerable effort. Holding his head up was a difficult affair.

The snake to his left collapsed to the turf and began writhing. One of Brinol's knives was imbedded in its eye. The other snake turned as fast as lightning toward its fallen brother. As is did so an arrow punched completely through its head to stick in the ground right next to Anric. That snake too, fell to the ground in convulsions.

He plucked the arrow from the ground. It was one from Dad's bow, and it was covered in green blood.

"Anric! Son, are you alright?" Dad yelled as he jumped from the wagon and ran toward him.

Anric was afraid to move, afraid that he might collapse if he took a step, so he just waited.

"What a fool thing to do. You could have been killed."

"That boy of yours is a fine student," the dwarf said as he walked toward them.

Dad turned toward the dwarf. There might have been an argument had not Mom screamed. They turned to her. She was running toward Lysa, who must have woken. Lysa was a sight. She looked awful. Her torn and bloody clothes didn't help.

"Is that Lysa Kairis?" Dad asked. He squinted at her.

Lysa's name awoke his purpose.

"Dad, I need you to take Lysa to Sadietown. Get to safety. Tell the guard that a maker is at Lifebringer."

Dad looked at him like he didn't know what he was.

"I've a horse over the hill to fit to the wagon."

Dad shook his head. Out in the field Mom was consoling Lysa. Brinol was doing some grisly work with the snake carcasses.

"You're coming with us, Anric," Dad said slowly, as if to make sure he understood every word.

"No," Anric said. "I have my own plans."

He could see the restrained tension in Dad's clenched fists.

"Anric, Jiles Morely is dead."

Anric frowned. Brinol grunted.

"He came to the farm holding his innards in with one hand. His other hand was off at the elbow. He said his wife had turned into some kind of giant lizard. He died right there on my threshold. I shot the monster that was following him with my bow a moment later."

Anric didn't know what to say to that, so he didn't say anything.

"Jiles was a beast of a man. I knew no man stronger. You're a fool if you go off monster hunting with this dwarf."

Anric glanced to Lysa, to the ruin that'd once been so beautiful.

"The horse is just over the hill. Good luck Father. I will catch up with you if I can." He turned from him and walked toward Lifebringer.

"Be smart, son," his father growled.

Anric ignored him and kept walking away.

"Get out of my way, dwarf," he heard his father say, though he still didn't turn around. He was afraid that if he turned around he might not do what he needed to do.

"Sounds, as if the lad's made up his mind, boyo," said the dwarf.

He heard a scuffle. He wanted to run away fast, get some distance, but thought that'd look immature. He was a man, doing a man's duty, and would not be made to feel like a child.

After a time the dwarf came trotting up to him on his big war horse.

"That falchion looks good in your hand, boy."

He'd not realized he still had the sword.

"Hand it to me and climb on up. I'll give it back to you if the need arises."

He looked up at the dwarf. Brinol was smiling down. His silver teeth were showing.

"You think me a fool, like my father?"

The dwarf shook his head. "Folk that say they're smart are usually the most fearful, I find. They hide behind their reasons. It lets them be cowards while keeping their conscious clear."

"I just want to help Lysa," he said.

The dwarf bent down and held out a hand. "There is no more noble a thing in this world."

Anric handed him the sword and Brinol boosted him up to sit behind him.

* * *

They made much quicker time without Anric's plow horse to slow them down. They rode briskly up and down the foothills, passing hilltop crops and valley homes. The grass was deep green despite the early season and cool weather. The whole area pulsed with vivid life, and it just got more intense as they neared the fabled Lifebringer spire.

Others were on the paths, all of them headed away. Anric saw many with bandages. The atrocities must not have been limited to only his and Mr. Morely's family.

"Brinol, what if these people have seeds like Mr. Morely had this morning?" Anric asked. They'd just passed a family with two young children, a boy and a girl. He shuddered to think what might happen to such a lovely new family if one of them had a seed.

Brinol, whose eyes seemed to be trying to see everything at once, growled. "Can't live that way boy. We got to kill the cause first and worry about the other later."

Anric looked up at the single, looming peak that was Lifegiver. "How are we going to find the maker, anyway? She could be anywhere."

"She'll find us boy. Have no fear. We're too much of a treat for her to pass up."

Anric didn't like the sound of that, so decided to keep his mouth shut while they made their quick way ever closer to the mountain's true slope.

* * *

By afternoon they'd crossed the foothills and had reached the first of the caves. As a boy he and his friends had gone inside a few, but never deep. The darkness inside was always just too much, no matter if they had a torch or not.

"Time to get off, boy," Brinol said. Anric dismounted, as did the dwarf.

Brinol took hold of his horse's bridal and looked hard into the beast's eye. "Stay," he said. "I'd as soon not take the chance of losing you."

The dwarf handed Anric the sword. "This is the place, boy. Steel that spine of yours."

Anric took the sword quick, lest Brinol feel his trembling grip.

"And this," he pulled a small, plugged gourd hanging on a chain from one of his pockets, "Is for collecting Lysa's medicine."

Anric took the gourd and rubbed its smooth side with a thumb.

"I hope this works," he said.

"Hope all you like," Brinol said, turning a full circle. He cupped his hands around his mouth. "I'm here, maker. Come if you dare!"

Silence followed his challenge.

"It may take a bit for the monster to find us," he said. "I'll give it a few then ask again." He nodded to the caves. "You know those supposedly lead to the heart of the mountain. Legend says Queen Krahain had quite the lair in there."

Brinol walked toward the closest of the caves and Anric followed. He didn't want the dwarf too far away.

"By the mines, I miss a good cave," Brinol said. "It does my soul good to get a taste of that wet limestone air. Be a lookout for all of a moment. I will return presently," he said. Before Anric could utter a complaint, the dwarf danced in a few steps and was lost in the deeper black of the cave.

The area around them was free of trees for a good stone's throw and the horse cropped grass not a few steps away, happy as can be. He could see no reason for worry. But still ...

"Are you sure this is a good idea?" he asked.

The dwarf didn't answer.

"Brinol?"

He heard what sounded like rocks clicking together then the sound of running feet. He jerked away from the cave entrance just as the dwarf's lower half came running out. A jagged red wound was all that remained of Brinol's upper half. The legs made it another few steps before tripping and falling onto the green grass, where they continued to piston in spasm.

The horse neighed and bolted. Anric stared. The rock clicking sound continued from deeper in the cave.

He needed to get out of here. Dad had been right. He couldn't help Lysa. It didn't matter how much he wanted to. He wasn't strong enough.

A tinkle of a laugh made his blood freeze. A little girl of maybe ten years stepped from another cave mouth just a few openings away. She wore a little floral dress of pink and yellow. Her hair was a mess of tangled black and grays. She looked skinny to the point of emaciation with arms and legs too long and spindly for her body. Her eyes though, her eyes were too perfectly round, and had too much white. The black at their center was tiny and dead looking.

He tried to move, but couldn't. His stomach was hot, like he was about to get sick. His knees hurt. His lower lip trembled. His mouth watered.

"Please," he said under his breath.

The little girl took her time walking closer. "Dwarves make the best bearers," she said. Her voice came out at two different pitches at the same time, one high, one low.

"But I'm not yet ready to tackle one." She tilted her head one way then the other, as if studying him.

"They're too hard, you see. Hard, hard, hard. Made of the mountain itself."

She was getting ever closer. His chest ached. He wanted to take a step back, just one, just to see if he could. But he didn't. All he could manage to do was shake his head.

"No," he said, his voice a little stronger than before.

She ignored him. "Rock biters love dwarf as well," she nodded toward the cave where the clinking sound continued, "but for a different reason than I."

It was chewing.

She smiled as she saw that he understood her meaning. Her teeth were all translucent slivers of needlepoint sharpness. Her mouth was so big it dominated more than half her face.

He glanced to the still twitching legs of Brinol. "No," he said, starting to cry.

"Why are you here?" she asked. She was very close now. Both her hands had nails thick and pointy enough to be called talons. In the center of either palm was a pulsating, yellow seed. They looked like infected abscesses ready to be lanced.

His nose was running and he sweated and trembled all over. He shook his head.

"Why would a frightened, little boy journey with a hard dwarf?"

She laid a sharp talon on the right side of his chest. He felt no pain, only a momentary coldness and pressure as she put a seed in him. Her dead eyes never left his.

"It doesn't matter," she said. "You are now a seed bearer," Her voice was more dark and guttural than before.

But it did matter. It had to matter.

His heart roared like it'd been kick started. The female maker's surprise was but a twitch as he swung the falchion with all his might. It imbedded into her left side deep enough to fully bury the metal.

"It matters," he spat in her evil face as she staggered back. "I'm scared. I'm afraid. I'm not strong at all!"

He ripped the sword out of her side and buried it in her skull. She jerked, her right hand going for the blade before she fell to her back.

He kicked her convulsing form over and over. "It matters." He loved Lysa and would do anything for her. Anything. It didn't matter if she loved him back or not.

* * *

He didn't know how long he kicked the now dead maker, but it was getting on toward evening. His chest where the monster had put the seed was numb to the touch and felt warm. He had to hurry. He pulled the plug from the gourd and filled it to the brim with reddish-purple blood.

Then he ran to Lysa. He ran as hard and as fast as he could.

Night fell and still he ran full out. He ran and did not tire. He ran and did not lose his breath.

His superhuman ability was a worry for another time. Lysa needed what he had. Her beauty should not be denied the world. He'd see it one more time, just once more. He'd be happy with that, just to see her smile.

Sadietown came in to view and he ran all the harder. He had no clue how he'd find her in the throng of people that'd surely be there seeking protection, and he did not care. He always seemed to find Lysa when he wanted to. It was like his soul had eyes that his body did not.

And he did find her. He walked to her without taking one single wrong step. She sat alone on a bench in an abandoned courtyard in a crosswalk between a couple of inns and daytime farmer storefronts. The moon had risen and was reflected in a square stone pool at the center of the intersection. He looked for his parents nearby, but there was nobody.

"Lysa," he said. His voice came out dry and hoarse. Now that he'd found her, he let himself relax, and in doing so the burning seed in his chest soared forth to almost consume his very being. He rammed it down, but just barely, and not without losing his legs. He fell to his knees.

His vision swam out of focus and then back in. Lysa was there. Her hands were like ice to the touch. He pulled the gourd from his pocket and handed it to her with violent, jerky shaking motions.

"Drink," he said and looked into her eyes. He tried to convey how important it was, but he could speak no more. Everything burned. The air was turning splotchy red. There was fear in Lysa's eyes. He wondered what she saw.

He closed his eyes and fought with all he had in order to stay whole as long as he could. She needed to get away now that she had her medicine. He focused on his heartbeat strumming loud and fitful in his ears.

Then he heard Lysa's sweet voice. But it wasn't anything he understood. She spoke the language of the fairy.

* * *

A soft hand touched his brow.

"The wickedness did not consume you," Lysa said.

His link to her, something that'd once always been a fragmented mess just under his consciousness, now felt deeper, felt harder and stronger. It was more accessible.

With an effort he opened his eyes. The moon remained as it'd been, as if no time at all had passed. Lysa smiled down at him from where he lay on the cobbled intersection. Even in the harsh, white moonlight her beauty was radiant. She was once again whole.

"You saved me," he said.

"We saved each other."

"But I feel..."

She shushed him. "Rest," she said.

He shook his head. He felt different all over, better on the inside. His doubt was gone, as was his fear. His spirit felt whole.

"You gave me something," he said, "something of yourself."

She nodded. "And you saved the world, the whole world."

He wondered if she knew how much he loved her. He'd not set out to save the world. All he'd wanted was to help her.

She laid a hand on his chest. "I know."

Life
Angela Acosta

Being trapped between this world and the next
is hardly a tight space.
It's an infinity in itself,
a nonzero integer
infinitesimally small
but powerful in nature.

A forever of nothing
pales in comparison
to the possibilities of now,
even as we obsess over lost time.

Two infinities surround us,
reminding us of the vastness of the cosmos
and the urgency to take pleasure in
dunking cookies into milk
with classmates at your professor's house
(and changing the subject).

For more where this came from, try "Summoning SpaceTravelers." Here's the ordering link: https://www.hiraethsffh.com/product-page/summoning-space-travelers-by-angela-acosta

Woman in the Moon
(Dedicated to Delonto Mae Relf)
Terrie Leigh Relf

The seductively sweet scent of oleander entranced and distracted me at the corner of Gramma's house where the magenta, mauve, and pink-tipped flowers bloomed in the moonlight. I touched a delicate petal. When I brought it close to my face to inhale its intoxicating fragrance, Gramma said, "Don't touch the Oleander -- it's poisonous! If you eat it, you'll lose your voice!"

"I'm not going to eat it, Gramma. Just smell it," I protested, amazed, even as a young girl, that something of beauty could be dangerous. I turned away from the flowers, away from the real or imagined threat of muteness.

Even though Gramma constantly reminded me that she was an old woman, she didn't look or seem elderly to me. Her waist-length blue-black hair cascaded down her back and over her shoulders; only a few strands of silver flowed through it.

"Let's walk around the block again," she said. At first, I hesitated, then wanting to please her, agreed.

I squirmed as we walked but she didn't seem to notice. I often wondered why she wanted me to walk with her when she was in one of her reflective moods, but then so much about Gramma was a mystery. "There's a woman in the moon," she said, while I covered my eyes in fear of the cold white light.

"OK, Gramma, there's a woman in the moon." A part of me wanted to believe her -- still wants to believe her -- but I now know that belief, like so many things in life—and death —is an elusive power.

Gramma had powers. Her son, my father, called them "dark." She called them "light." I often felt that there was but a horizon's edge that separated one from the other. "You're a lot like me," Gramma would often say, and then become unusually still.

I shivered, feeling the moon's cold stare as I took one step and then another down the block. Sometimes I would try to count my steps, but I would often become distracted and forget what number I was on. How many steps had I taken with Gramma? Could I ever count that high?

As we neared the next corner, Gramma stopped in front of a familiar house, turned to me, and said, "You remember Lenore, don't you, Lily? This is where she lived," Gramma said, pointing toward a small cottage with an unkempt yard, where flowers lay without their sweet nectar, trampled by a recent rain.

While Gramma was reminiscing aloud, Lenore appeared in the front window, seated in a dark-green velvet chair, a grey Persian cat on her lap, its tail furled around the book she read. Sensing our presence, she set down the book she was reading and rose slightly from her chair in greeting. Her cat leapt gracefully from her lap onto the windowsill, watching us through the window with iridescent eyes.

Passing the next yard, Gramma nodded to a man watering his roses across the street. Their eyes met, rested for a moment, then seemed to part reluctantly. He reminded me of a photograph on Gramma's piano, someone she had known long ago, someone I sensed she loved. I turned around to see if he watched our passage, but he—and his roses—had gone.

As we continued our walk, Gramma occasionally paused in front of someone's house, tilting her head towards it, listening. It was a while, though, before she stopped for longer than a moment or two and spoke.

"And you remember Bernice, don't you dear? How I miss our card games!"

Gramma leaned against the fence in front of Bernice's house. A strand of ivy reached for and clung to her hand. She removed it gently, so as not to break the stem, then sighed, "How I miss my friends."

Out of the corner of my eye, I watched as Bernice appeared the door, holding the screen open just far enough to beckon us inside.

I shivered again, feeling a familiar call, from whom I wasn't sure.

"You should have brought a sweater," Gramma said, as if a sweater's warmth could protect against this penetrating chill.

We came to the empty lot just around the corner from Gramma's house where I had spent so many afternoons alone. I would lie on my back, watch the play of light and shadow through the overhanging branches of the lone Pepper tree. Oftentimes, I would roll the mauve-brown peppercorns between my fingers, imagining that they were magic.

Gramma wanted to walk some more, but this time she wanted to walk towards the ocean. "It's so beautiful at night," she said.

Longing to return to the house but unsure what would happen once we arrived, I shielded my face and eyes from the moon's presence. Gramma pulled my arm down.

"Look!" She pointed at the moon. I felt courageous for a moment, until I noticed how the moon's visage shined full upon me.

Sensing my concern, Gramma said, "Don't worry about it, dear -- she will guide and protect you."

"Who?" I asked, believing then as I do even now that Gramma was the only one who could take care of me, that she had been the one to bring me over when I drowned. I moved closer to her, reached for her hand as we neared the beach. The closer we came to the boardwalk, the tighter I held onto her.

"The grunion are running," someone had said earlier, and I remember wanting to see the silvery bodies undulating in the moonlight, burrowing deep into the sand, their eggs foaming from their bodies like the froth of a wave. Did they really exist, or were they part of someone's dream?

The tides were high due to a sudden storm, but it was low tides that frightened me because they uncovered what was usually hidden.

I watched a wave as it neared shore, thinking how beautifully it swelled and peaked, curving around and under itself. Even as it tugged at my feet and the silvery sand gave way beneath me, I thought of how it would feel to be held in its embrace.

The water was cold, brutally cold, so I imagined that I was a seal playing out beyond the breakers, rolling over and under the surface with each oncoming wave, and then that I was a mischievous mermaid, playing hide-and-seek with my Selkie sisters far out beyond the storm-thrashed breakers.

But I grew tired of my fanciful thoughts and rolled over onto my back to gaze full upon my first Blue Moon. I was in awe of her beauty resonating across the wide expanse of an indigo sky, her hair alight with stars which I traced with an imaginary hand, unable to lift my own. A curious tugging began in my lower abdomen and then a cold heat coursed through me, exploding into a brilliant light. From somewhere far away, I heard a haunting melody, so exquisitely beautiful that my eyes began to tear. I followed the sound and saw an old woman lifting a fragile form from its nest of tangled seaweed fronds and driftwood limbs. She held the child close against her, then leaned back into the water, disappearing from view.

"You're dreaming again," Gramma said, gently shaking my shoulder. I remembered times when she would tuck me into bed at night, pulling the warm flannel sheets up to my chin, followed by a series of multi-colored Afghans that she had crocheted with my Great Grandmother and Great Aunts. Before turning out the light, Gramma would place a rouged kiss upon my forehead and say, "Sweet dreams and no worries—goodnight."

"Don't forget my night-light, Gramma," I would reply.

"The moon will light your way, sweetie," Gramma would always respond.

I wanted to believe that her simple spells would work, that nightmares would vanish once they were remembered, and that the horrors within them were like stars, an intense but faraway light.

But I know differently now.

I awoke in the middle of the night and Gramma was kneeling at the side of my bed whispering something in my ear. When she saw that I was awake, she said, "Go back to sleep, Lily, it's late."

"Then why'd you wake me, Gramma?" I yawned sleepily.

"I just wanted to see you again," she said softly, "before I go."

"OK Gramma, g'night."

In the morning, the aroma of lemon and poppy seed muffins roused me from sleep.

"Good morning, sleepy-head," she smiled as I sat down at the table, watching her smear butter on hot muffins.

"I had the strangest dreams last night, Gramma."

She paused, set down the butter knife, placed her palms together, collecting her thoughts.

"Dreams are like the layers of the onion. When you peel each layer away, there's another and then another, and still another layer," Gramma said.

"But then there's nothing left," I responded, perplexed. But Gramma just smiled at my confusion.

"No, Lily, there's more. So much more."

We continued to eat muffins and sip Earl Grey tea in a comforting silence. After a time Gramma said, "Are you ready to go back now?"

She knew the answer before she asked, but Gramma always said that I had a choice. I knew that my family might miss me. I had a few friends, too, but what I really wanted was to stay with Gramma at her house forever.

"Okay, I'll go back . . . but Gramma?"

"Yes, Lily?"

"I always knew you'd find a way to visit me after you'd gone, but I never thought it would be like this."

Gramma laughed heartily, throwing her head back, nearly losing her balance in the shifting sand.

"Will I ever see you again, Gramma?"

"Perhaps—" her voice trailed off as she turned to search the sky over the horizon's edge, the moon a pale grey in the approaching dawn.

"Let's walk a bit longer, Lily. The living can always wait."

Movie review:
Everything Everywhere All at Once
Lee Clark Zumpe

Can someone please explain when and how multiverse movies became mainstream? Seriously: Wasn't the many-worlds interpretation of quantum mechanics – with its myriad universes – a concept that only surfaced in media targeting sci-fi afficionados until fairly recently?

In 2022, the idea of parallel dimensions and universe-jumping hit the big screen in an American independent film that has altered the cinematic landscape. Directed by Daniel Kwan and Daniel Scheinert, "Everything Everywhere All at Once" began as a limited theatrical release, opening in select theaters on March 25. A one-night IMAX release followed. Because of the film's popularity, it was rereleased in July, reaching a wider audience. After garnering 11 Oscar nominations, it was again rereleased on Jan. 27, 2023.

Even before "Everything Everywhere All at Once," moviegoers had been exposed to many recent cinematic representations of the multiverse, in films such as "Spider-Man: No Way Home," and "Doctor Strange in the Multiverse of Madness," and in streaming series such as Netflix's "The Umbrella Academy" and Marvel's "Loki" on Disney+. But "Everything Everywhere All at Once" differs from all these productions in one important regard: It's not just another comic-book spawned superhero-centric story.

Michelle Yeoh stars as Evelyn Wang, a frustrated and unsatisfied immigrant mother and business owner. At a time when she is juggling a dozen responsibilities, she is approached by someone from a parallel universe who claims only she can save the multiverse from an impending catastrophe.

Evelyn isn't a conventional hero. She doesn't even qualify as the reluctant hero archetype — at least not in the traditional sense. At one point in the film, her recruiter reveals to her that she was chosen because, unlike all the other versions of her, she is unique in that she lacks any functional skill set. While all the other Evelyns have excelled at *something*, she fails at *everything*. Her life is a string of disadvantageous choices, poorly executed undertakings, and abandoned dreams. She is a *tabula rasa* in terms of her potential.

Evelyn's husband Waymond Wang, played by Ke Huy Quan, attempts to pacify his wife's overriding sense of persistent failure with tender compassion. Her daughter, Joy Wang (Stephanie Hsu), is desperate to elicit any sign of affection from Evelyn. Because her efforts have gone largely unnoticed, Joy is starting to succumb to her mother's bleak worldview.

In Evelyn's universe, Deirdre Beaubeirdre (Jamie Lee Curtis) is her primary adversary. Deirdre, an IRS auditor, is exasperated with Evelyn's inability to properly file her taxes and is preparing to seize her laundromat over unpaid taxes.

The threat to the multiverse comes from Jobu Tupaki – an alternate version of Joy. Mired in nihilistic ontology, she has constructed a ravenous singularity that encompasses literally everything that has, does, and will exist throughout all the infinite universes. The very existence of this black hole-like "everything bagel," as Jobu calls it, threatens to disintegrate all spacetime.

Despite her initial attempts to avoid the call to adventure, Evelyn gradually becomes entangled in the struggle. She is exposed to a dizzying array of alternate realities through "verse-jumping" technology, which she uses to glimpse universes in which she has found success, fame, and wealth. She is able to acquire the abilities of her counterparts, which she then uses to defend herself against enemy agents and to try to delay a direct confrontation with Jobu.

"Everything Everywhere All at Once" relies upon kaleidoscopic visuals, emotional storytelling, powerful performances, and technical wizardry. The filmmakers blend science fiction, wuxia, absurdist fiction, and comedy-drama, creating a spectacular and surreal journey exploring the depths of human suffering, and revealing how and endless procession of trivial distractions can cause us to lose sight of what is important in our lives.

If Edward Albee had ever written about Lovecraftian horrors, I think it would look a lot like "Everything

Everywhere All at Once." Jobu's singularity subverts the concept of the existential void: Instead of the horror of nothingness, she imagines the horror of an infinite *everythingness*. They notions are two sides of the same philosophical coin. If existence is an endless panorama of every potential reality, then nothing has significance. Except, of course, it does, as Evelyn finally realizes.

Yeoh's performance is everything it needs to be, and more. She provides the anchor the viewer needs to weather this cinematic maelstrom. Quan is equally brilliant, and Hsu's contrasting portrayal of Joy and Jobu shows her dramatic range.

"Everything Everywhere All at Once" is the kind of film that requires unbroken attention. It is challenging, intense, and exasperating — and equally mesmerizing and gratifying. Kwan and Scheinert accurately portray the nightmarish nonsense of everyday chaos, evoking wonder, confusion, and empathy. The film is a tribute to personal sacrifice, and to fleeting moments of profound clarity when we experience a life-defining epiphany.

INFO BOX
"Everything Everywhere All at Once"
Genres: Everything
Directors: Daniel Kwan and Daniel Scheinert
Cast: Michelle Yeoh, Stephanie Hsu, Ke Huy Quan, Jenny Slate, Harry Shum Jr., James Hong, and Jamie Lee Curtis
Release date: March 25, 2022
Run time: 139 minutes
Rated: R

She Makes Narcissus Bloom
Lisa Voorhees

Evening had descended in the Underworld, the skies painted a chalky gray without a single thundercloud threatening the horizon. For Hades, nothing could compare to eating out on the terrace in such fine weather as this.

In the dim light of the first underground level, Persephone's fair skin glowed behind the rich red velvet of her gown, her dark hair framing a contemplative, slightly forlorn, expression. Hades had grown to dread the recent sadness that had swelled inside those honey-colored eyes.

Persephone had been sixteen when he'd first met her and delivered her to the Underworld in his golden carriage. She was fully a woman now, their lives measured more by the rhythmic tide of wraith-like souls traveling through to the deeper levels below than by any accounting of mortal years.

They were immortal, fully god and goddess. Though Persephone was technically a lesser deity than he, the distinction had never been important to Hades. It was Persephone's generosity of spirit he couldn't live without, her genuine acceptance of the entirety of who he was, where the other Olympians were quick to scorn him.

Hades wiped his mouth and set his napkin beside his empty plate, noting the amount of pomegranate wine left in his wife's pewter goblet.

Persephone had taken to leaving her wine mostly untouched these days, a fact which disturbed Hades, while at the same time he hesitated to point it out to her. He was under no illusions about how much Persephone longed to use her gift the way she once had.

While the distillation of the pomegranate seeds increased her attachment to him and to the Underworld, it also had the less than desirable effect of blunting her regenerative gift to produce flowers in all their infinite array of tones and colors. That, he knew, was the price she paid for remaining with him in the Underworld.

He hardly dared to ask what thoughts ran through her mind. Did they lead her away from him, or drive her deeper into a reason for staying? He knew she loved him, as he loved her, but his heart quailed at the faraway look on her face.

A sleek vulture landed on the stone balustrade next to Persephone. The creature cocked a gleaming black eye at the fleshy remains of roast pheasant on the china plate before her.

"Of course, Templeton," she said, tossing out a meaty bone. With a clack, the bird's beak snapped around the treat; it launched off the balustrade and glided to the garden floor to feast in solitude.

"They have grown to love you," Hades said. "You are good to them."

Persephone smiled into the distance. "They are easy to love," she said quietly. "They expect so little and give so much in return." She turned to him, though her smile was not reflected in her eyes.

Such sadness lingered there. How he longed to eradicate it, though not enough to remove her wine glass from the table. His fear of losing her sank deeper than that.

He watched as his wife's gaze trailed over the garden, pausing at the circular bed of narcissus surrounding the central stone pool. At the sight of the flowers, her power rose within her, eliminating the sadness from her honey eyes and transforming her from the inside out.

Persephone labored, her eyes sealed shut, her hands lifted slightly off her lap. A glimmering iridescence crept up the stems of the narcissus flowers and flowed through the silken white petals, illuminating the cup shaped structures in the middle.

She sank back in her seat with a sigh, her energies expended. The narcissus gleamed a bright, amplified white long afterward.

"Enchanting, my dear," Hades said, admiring her work. "The transformation you have wrought in the Underworld continues to astonish me. Persephone–"

"Hades, please don't." She pressed her lips together and turned away from him. "My gift is...as underdeveloped as it is, I am determined to learn the true purpose for it, and how I can best put it to use."

Stay with me here in the Underworld, cultivating beauty and new life wherever the touch of your gift happens to alight, Hades thought. He could not bring himself to speak the words aloud, for fear of the conflict that even now warred inside Persephone's heart.

A servant in black livery stepped through the French doors and approached Hades with a whispered message.

The god inclined his head in receipt of the news. He pushed back his chair with a glance at Persephone. "Excuse me." He gave her a quick smile.

He crossed the dining room and entered the main hallway. Dusky light spilled onto the interlocking stone tiles, dimly illuminating the face of the griffon statue that guarded the bottom of the winding staircase.

Hades climbed the stairs and traversed the familiar warren of darkened hallways to his study. Once there, he closed the heavy mahogany door behind him and hurried to his desk. He opened the lowest drawer on the right, lifted the false bottom, and reached for the sealed letter on top of a stack of similarly sized letters.

The wax bore Demeter's imprint, sheaves of wheat laid overtop a sickle. Persephone's mother sent the messages on the first evening of each new moon. He slid his finger below the wax, prepared to break the seal, when a knock sounded at the door.

"Who is it?" Hades asked.

The door creaked open. In the half light of the hallway, the shadows lining the folds of Persephone's gown deepened to claret, like a wine stain long seeped into the carpet.

Her face was pale and colorless. Her gaze fell to the letter in his hands.

"What is that you're about to read?"

Hades tucked the paper behind his back. "An accounting issue, that is all."

"Do not lie to me, husband. I know when something worries you."

Hades mustered a grim smile. "It is nothing that need concern you. All is well, Persephone."

He hoped to reassure her by his tone, but she proceeded further inside his study. She took a seat on the worn green velvet armchair by the fireplace, her gaze shifting vacantly between the twin gargoyles flanking the mantel.

When she turned to him, her honey colored eyes shone wet with unshed tears. "May I ask you something?"

"Anything you wish."

She continued to stare at him, as if weighing the effect of her unspoken words against whatever she observed in his expression. Gently, Persephone folded her hands in her lap, the decorative points of her sleeves trailing against her skirts.

"The carriage," she said stiffly. "I believe the rear axle is cracked from disuse. Will you have someone take a look at it?"

After that pronouncement, she rose and exited the room, closing the door behind her.

Hades furrowed his brows. If Persephone had designs on leaving the Underworld, fixing the carriage would be the way to go about it. Yet out of respect, she'd approached him first rather than taken care of it quietly behind his back. The thought weighed heavily on him as he broke the seal on the missive before him and read:

Hades,

My dearest hope is that you have not cast these letters aside. Please hear me out, and do not add to a suffering mother's grief the further wound of your contempt regarding my pleas.

My daughter has seen fit to spend more seasons in the Underworld than she, or you, have any right to detain her. The coming harvest season will mark a full year since her last appearance in the mortal realm.

Earth cannot sustain another winter such as this past one before resources become scarce and humans perish needlessly.

Though I control the harvest, my power alone is insufficient to raise flowers from the ground. Persephone's unique skill with flowering life is required for the fields to flourish, and for Earth as mortals know it to continue to prosper.

This new moon marks the start of the next planting cycle. I beg you to release Persephone from your grasp according to the schedule dictated by Olympus: two-thirds of the year on Earth, one-third of the year in the Underworld. If you continue to defy the mandates of Zeus, he will act in my favor to ensure her return.

Yours,
Demeter

With a sigh, Hades allowed the letter to fall from his hand onto the desk. Before it grew any later and night descended, he needed to make a visit. Persephone's question about the faulty axle nagged at him. His restless heart stirred within him, plagued with the recurring question of what extremes he would go to in order to keep Persephone with him in the Underworld.

He placed the letter on top of the others in the secret compartment, closed the drawer, and left his study. The halls of the manor house were deathly quiet at this time of the evening; at no point did he encounter either Persephone or any of the servants.

Hades exited by way of the rear doors, delivering him directly into the gardens. Overhead, the terrace stood empty. After speaking with him, Persephone must have chosen to retire to their chambers.

Perched on the branches of the snaggy dead trees, the vultures lounged with wings outspread and wrinkled heads cocked at an angle, eyeballing him. He paused before the stone pool and stared into its black depths, the surface of the water slick and smooth, as if coated by an oily sheen.

When a message was important enough, the surface would break apart and give him a vision of Earth, or of Olympus, though the gods rarely resorted to communicating this way with him anymore. Their messages went largely unheeded and the pool had sat, undisturbed, for more years than Hades could count.

He bent down for a closer look at the narcissus flowers. The brightest creation inside the Underworld, and they were all Persephone's doing. Hades ran a finger along one petal and cupped the flower in his palm.

Such tender life she had coaxed from the barren soil of the Underworld, using her unique power. Persephone was his winter flower, the white bloom of his immortal, darkened soul, the narcissus that flowered year round, on Earth as it did in the Underworld. Her ability to produce life where none existed previously not only fascinated him, it had become his lifeblood, the ticking rhythm of his heart, the guiding force of his days, and the joyful comfort of his nights.

She had awoken his very soul, in a way he had not thought possible prior to experiencing the force of her love.

He continued along the winding path through the gardens and out the back gate. A gravel path led through a thick forest of sagging pines to the vineyard at the westernmost portion of the estate.

Hades passed orderly rows of grapevines and pomegranate trees laden with dark, ripened fruit and twisted leaves. He approached the thatch roofed cottage of the head winemaker and rapped once on the door with his knuckles.

"Mihalis," he said, and at the sound of his voice, a white haired, bespectacled man in a worn apron glanced up from his exacting work with a charcoal stick, recording various figures in a wide ledger.

The man scrambled to his feet, unbalancing his stool, which crashed to the floor behind him. "My lord," he said, inclining his head and pressing his hands together over his chest. "How can I be of service?"

"What vintage of pomegranate wine was last delivered to the house?"

"Only the one you requested, sir, the thousands' year old. The Byzantine autumnal stock, of which there's plenty enough to last for weeks yet, provided it's only you and my lady partaking."

"I would like you to provide us with something stronger."

"M-more potent than the Byzantine, my lord?"

Hades nodded.

"The only stock older than that dates back to Origin times. The soil was hardly more than ash and limestone. I fear the wine will be–"

"Those are my wishes." Hades did not turn his gaze from Mihalis. His heart burned within him like a smoldering coal. Only the oldest wine the Underworld had produced would be capable of weaving a tighter spell around Persephone, binding her to the land, and ultimately to him. Tendrils of smoke lifted off of his dark clothing.

Before him, Mihalis trembled. He ran a hand over the displaced wisps of hair on his head. "V-very well, my lord. The Origin vintage it is."

"It is a matter of great importance," Hades said. "You will do as I command."

"Of course. I am your faithful servant always." Mihalis bowed his head and shuffled away in the direction of the cellars.

Heavy, leaden rain fell from the skies the next morning. After breakfast, Persephone went to the library to read and Hades had come to his study to finish looking over some paperwork, or so he had told her.

Every candelabra had been lit. The flames leapt and sputtered with the draft entering from the crack under the door. Hades squeezed his forehead against his palms. The truth was, he was beginning to doubt he had the means of keeping Persephone with him at all.

Her admiration of him had been evident since the beginning, when he'd first noticed her among the flowers in the fields, working alongside her mother. In the light of the Earth's sun, his golden glow had transfixed her. She'd known he was a god and submitted to his intentions as soon as he'd invited her to step inside the golden carriage.

Contrary to his expectation, she had adapted easily to his more formidable appearance in the Underworld: his extraordinary height, and the shadowy darkness of his countenance. Neither the eccentricities of his habits, the barrenness of the landscape, nor the traveling souls making their descent into the depths of the levels below had prevented her from staying with him, winter after winter.

He fell madly in love with her and, as she grew to womanhood, he reveled in the dawning awareness that her affection for him had blossomed into something far deeper. They were truly god and goddess, rulers of the underground realms, though Persephone shrank from the distinction when he spoke of it.

"You consider me too highly," she said, and he had demurred, plying her instead with tender reassurances.

When she expressed her dismay at having to leave to go aboveground a year ago, he'd reached for the pomegranate wine out of desperation, believing that her unspoken plea was to be released from the responsibility Demeter and the other gods had enforced upon her.

Persephone had chosen to stay, applying her efforts, in particular, to the garden. The narcissus she had cultivated were vivid proof of where her heart's true bounty lay.

Weren't they?

These tortured thoughts, they did him no good. Try as he might, he could not discern her intentions any more than he could probe the most hidden recesses of her heart.

A knock at the door interrupted his mind's wanderings.

"Yes?"

A servant entered and delivered a letter on a silver tray. After a quick bow, he left.

Hades noted the insignia on the wax seal; a lightning bolt, this time. He pitched forward in his seat, nearly dropping the letter.

Carefully, he loosened the seal, opened the letter, and read the contents.

H,

You're not fooling anyone. Everyone notices Persephone's absence during the warm seasons and our sister is beside herself.

Let's not give Demeter any reason to complain to Olympus about our arrangement, shall we? It was a good and fair one, in my honest opinion, provided everyone plays by the rules.

No need to reply unless you consider it necessary; Persephone's appearance will be sufficient.

Do play along, brother. I'd hate to send Hermes to do the fetching. No one wants that.

Z.

Hades set the letter on the desk and groaned. He could already feel a headache coming on.

Dinner was a delicious affair: the cook's special roast lamb served with tzatziki and stuffed eggplant. True to his word, Mihalis had delivered the Origin vintage to the kitchen earlier that afternoon. With delight, Hades noted how eagerly Persephone downed one cupful after another, the servants liberally refilling her goblet with a fresh pour as soon as she had drained the last one.

"Is the food to your liking?" He skewered a piece of eggplant, but kept his eye on Persephone as he asked.

She had avoided conversation with him for much of the day, which added to his surprise at the vigor of her appetite. Persephone had a delicate constitution. When she was worried, it affected her whole person, and most particularly her digestion.

If she was eating this well, she must have reached some sort of decision. About what, he had no way of knowing unless he asked her.

"Yes, it's delicious," she said. "Cook has done a wonderful job."

There was no trace of hesitation in her statement. The compliment was genuine, as was her enjoyment of the meal. He would have to probe further. "I am sorry we could not eat on the terrace," he said. "It was much too wet after the rains earlier today."

"We should take a walk in the gardens after dessert. It is not too damp for that," she said, resting her honey-colored eyes on him.

He read satisfaction there, as he would expect after several goblets of the strongest pomegranate wine the Underworld could produce, and yet there was more. Her previous restlessness had strengthened into a type of resolve.

The knot of anxiety in his stomach tightened. He sensed she was prepared to speak to him about what was on her mind.

They finished their baklava and made their way to the garden via the lower entrance. By the side of the stone pool, they stopped.

A rustling in the trees attracted Persephone's attention. She glanced up among the branches, giving a delighted "oh!" as a black-winged vulture sailed through the air toward her outstretched arm. Persephone pulled back her head.

Talons extended, flapping awkwardly to slow his descent, the bird landed on her forearm, drew in his wings, and turned himself around. Stringy feathers sprigged from his gnarled head; he tipped a wise, beady eye in her direction.

"Irving," she cooed at him. "Always a pleasure, my sweet." He lowered his head and she drew her fingertips down the sleek feathers along his spine. The bird pressed his wizened head against her cheek and Persephone leaned into him, closing her eyes.

Gods, she was a beautiful creature, his Persephone. He loved watching her enjoyment of the vultures and her ease among the treasures in their garden, not to mention her joy at bringing the narcissus to life and enhancing the color of the flowers: a different luminescent shade every day, according to her whims.

It seemed the Origin vintage was working. Persephone was more at peace than he'd seen her for weeks, months even. Though Hades preferred not to keep an accounting of time in the manner of mortals, the steady accumulation of Demeter's letters reinforced just how long Persephone had chosen to remain with him in his kingdom.

He would have to ask Mihalis how much of that vintage remained in the cellars. If he could keep Persephone with him throughout this harvest season, it would be winter soon enough and then, at least, the gods could not bother him with their incessant letters and increasing threats. He could care less about the upheaval he was causing with Olympus and on Earth; he cared only inasmuch as his actions would influence Persephone's decision to stay in the Underworld, and to rule beside him as his queen.

Irving joined the rest of his flock among the trees and Persephone accompanied Hades in a walk around the stone pool. As they passed the stables and the small outbuilding where his chariot was stored, she made no remark. Her gaze lingered briefly on the structure before she brought the back of his hand to her mouth and kissed it, pressing it to her cheek afterward.

At the feel of her warmth against his skin, his heart swelled. Surely he could place his confidence in the fulness of the wine's effect.

They took a seat on the pool's edge. The darkening skies overhead had cleared to an ashen gray, lending the surface of the pool a steely, mercury-like glint.

"Are you happy here?" Hades asked. "With me?"

Persephone took his hand between both of hers and squeezed it. "Yes, of course. How could you imagine otherwise?"

Before he could reply, he sensed movement in the inky black waters, a shifting of the sky's reflection on the mirror-like surface. Swirls of silver resolved into snow encrusted trees, their branches laden with ice. The vision swept outward to include acres of desolate fields and windswept land, devoid of crops or any natural life beyond the wintry, beleaguered forest.

Persephone pulled her hands away from his and turned to stare at it. Her chest rose and fell, her eyes widening as realization hit her.

"Hades, what's happening?" She pointed a finger at the pool. "Is this a vision of Earth? Gods, it...the land looks so dead. The fields are frozen and lifeless."

Hades stood up, mortified at the activity taking place in the waters that had, until now, stayed so quiet and peaceable. What had he done wrong? The wine had worked, he was certain it had.

He wanted to dash his hand against the water and erase the nightmare taking place before his eyes.

Persephone leaned forward, spellbound.

"We should go inside," he said, extending a hand toward her. "Come with me."

She brushed him off, scooting along the stones and continuing to stare at the images playing out before them.

"I don't understand any of it," he continued. "We should leave."

"I think I do," she said. "Hades, this is a vision of Earth if I do not return to help...oh gods, look." Her voice had dropped. "Someone is coming!"

Hades took one glance at the newly clouded appearance of the waters and wished he never had. Slowly, as if emerging from the ether of Olympus itself, the face of a god materialized on the surface of the pool, a winged helmet on his head. He bore a winged staff in his grip.

"It's Hermes," Persephone breathed.

Hades lifted her up, placing himself between her and the pool in order to wrench her gaze from the waters. "It's not real," he said. "None of it. The pool cannot be trusted."

Persephone twisted out of his grasp and flew back to the water's edge. "No!" she cried. "I believe it is true! Hades, we cannot go on this way anymore."

"What way?"

"Keeping secrets from each other. I cannot stand it." She turned to face him, withdrew a folded paper from inside her sleeve, and held it aloft between them, her eyes wild and desperate, pleading with him. "This. This is what I mean."

As she spoke, the paper dropped open, revealing Demeter's words, her signature at the bottom of the letter.

"How long do you expect me to keep ignoring who I am? To turn a blind eye to my mother's entreaties?"

Hades was flabbergasted. Persephone had been in his study, riffling through his papers? She must have discovered the secret compartment, but when? How many of her mother's letters had she seen? He reached for the parchment and she snatched it away and slid it inside her sleeve.

"Where did you get that? That letter is not addressed to you."

Persephone bit her lip and glared sideways at the ground. "It doesn't matter. You shouldn't have kept it from me."

"I was afraid," he said, his gut twisting at the admission. With anyone but Persephone, he would never have exposed such a weakness inside himself.

"I have to return to Earth," Persephone said, her eyes afire.

"Demeter is far more powerful than she lets on," he replied. "She can handle the season changes by herself."

"It was never a question of her power. Her grief at my absence is what hinders her, and what endangers mankind as a result."

Hades retreated inside himself. What objection could he make in response? The heads of the narcissus flowers swayed in a light breeze. He stared at them until his eyes burned from their brightness.

"Zeus will not hesitate to send Hermes," she said. "The waters are proof of that. He may be on his way already."

Hades could not bring himself to look her in the eye.

"I have wrestled with this decision for the past year," Persephone continued. "I cannot tell you how hard it has been."

"I sensed it."

"I am sorry, Hades."

"I have defied Olympus before. I am not bound by their rules."

"But I am. There are consequences we cannot disregard."

"For Demeter, you mean? And mortals? What are they to me? They despise me."

Persephone reached for his hands and pressed his fingers to her lips. A warm tear slid through his palm, coming to rest on his wrist. "I do not despise you. I never have. Hades..."

He held her against him and kissed her head.

When she drew back, he saw the torment in her eyes. "This decision now requires no less courage on my part than stepping inside your chariot all those years ago. Neither one falls outside the boundaries of the goddess I am meant to be. It is my progression, nothing more, and certainly nothing less."

"I have grown accustomed to your presence. The Underworld is yours, and all that is mine within it."

A pained look crossed her face. "This is my home, Hades, as Earth is my duty."

"You will be gone for so long."

She took a moment before she replied. "Will you allow me to go? I do not seek your permission, though I would ask for your blessing."

"I will not keep you, but I beg you to stay."

Her hands slid away from his and she gave a small nod. He watched as her gaze lifted to the trees. The vultures lurked within the shelter of the gnarled branches, afraid to expose themselves as if aware of the dispute taking place in the garden below and seeking to remain hidden from it.

He witnessed her sigh and the ensuing set of jaws as she braced herself for what was to come.

Persephone approached the darkened pool, waded through the bed of narcissus, and stepped up onto the stone rim. She glanced over her shoulder at him, her half smile the last thing he remembered seeing before she plummeted into the inky depths, the quickest way for her to travel aboveground to Earth short of being escorted by a winged Olympian messenger.

One second with him, the next vanished, her solitary dried tear the only remnant of her presence with him the moment before.

She had claimed the Underworld as her home, but who was to say what tricks the gods would play once she returned to Earth? They were as capable of keeping her from returning to him during the winter as he was of persuading her to stay in the Underworld past the agreed upon intervals.

His flagrant disavowal of the terms that had been laid down could be the seed of his future undoing.

Yet Persephone had made her own choice.

He had wanted her to. She had a right to her freedom, much as the agony of it pierced his soul.

A dreadful tiredness settled over him, leaching into his bones and draining him of energy for his usual pursuits. Already, the air seemed more dead, the flowers less startlingly white, the vultures silent captives in the surrounding trees.

Hades left the garden and returned to the manor house. He passed the griffon statue guarding the hallway and wound his way up the flight of stairs and through the drafty hallways to their chambers.

The heavy damask curtains covered the windows and, in his dark mood, he was tempted to leave them closed. A peculiar smell wafted past his nose: an earthen freshness, a heady aroma that both set his heart to thrumming and his mind into denial that what he sensed could be real.

He pulled the cord on the curtains and opened them, allowing the sparse gray light to spill across the room.

Along every crevice on the edges of the floor, narcissus flowers bloomed. The longer he watched, the more appeared: at the base of the furniture, the window ledges, and even sprouting from the sides of the bed.

Hades stood still, absorbing the spectacle before him. The last flower to emerge grew from the center of his pillow.

He watched it blossom and shimmer a brilliant, dazzling white, the central cup opening and flaring, offering all of itself even in the dim light of the Underworld.

Rattling Bones on the Black River
Ethan Robles

Undvik tossed two handfuls of dirt onto his son's face before he lost control. Kier was dead, his body drained of its blood. His stark white flesh stood out in the dark earth.

As Undvik waded into grief, Duval pushed the remainder of the dirt into the grave. The grim labor made him sweat through his clothes. When it was done, he patted the dirt and rose from the ground. Undvik was off near the tree line. He sobbed quiet tears. Seeing the filled grave, he wandered over. He laid his hands on the soil and splayed his fingers out. He wanted to feel his son beneath him, but all he felt was the ground, still wet with recent rain.

"It's time to go." Duval said.

He affixed his axe to his belt and pulled his furs over his shoulders. The sky threatened to rain again. The storm would soon drench them both if they didn't get under cover. He would be prepared.

"What was it that took him?" Undvik said. The pale herb-master had only known his chemicals, his plants. His sword arm was weak. He'd learned little of the world beyond his laboratory.

"I don't know."

Duval turned back toward the path. They'd given up precious time. The sun rose and set behind a cloudy, gray sky. The dull, diffused glow told him that it would be night soon. They had not set a camp. They'd not found dried wood for their fire. Nor had they managed to scavenge any food from the forest floor. The tangled expanse they traversed offered few chances to hunt. They had become accustomed to dining on the insects they could trap between their fingers.

"You killed it!" Undvik said. His anger helped him rise from his son's resting place. Duval was thankful for the man's rage. It would keep the herb-master moving through the worst leg of their journey. "How does a man not know what he kills?"

"It is not like pulling a plant from the ground, Undvik." Duval tapped one finger on the axe head that clung to his belt. He needed the herb-master. Needed his strange mixtures. "It's not like crushing a weed with your mortar and pestle. I don't have time to categorize the things that live in the wild. You've had a convenient life. It's time that you knew that."

Undvik looked shocked. His mourning had sunken his eyes deeper into his head. He'd not slept and the dark circles above his cheeks were spotted with dirt, his face spattered with the same soil that covered his son. An old man pulled from the town that housed him, pushed into the wild with a mercenary on a mission he barely understood. Duval wanted to feel sympathy for the man. But he only felt frustration.

"It's time to go, Undvik." Duval said, lightening his voice a little. "The sun is going down and we will be left in the dark without a fire. Could be rain, too. There are worse things than what killed Kier. I hope to not find them."

Undvik seemed to understand. He nodded slowly and looked back at the grave. As he walked away, he continued to look back at his son, his apprentice. The boy had volunteered to go, so excited he was to see the world beyond his hamlet. And now he would never return. His body would decay below moist earth. A feast for the things that tunneled under their feet.

As they walked, Duval thought of the thing that took Kier's life. He'd seen nothing like it. He'd traveled through the worst of the boglands, the deserts. His fate was to be moving beneath the gray sky. An axe for hire. He'd wandered into Krakenhom after he'd split from a traveling party. They'd taken to contract killing and petty assassination. Duval had few scruples, but he found himself disgusted at the thought of killing unsuspecting targets. Exterminating monsters in the wild was one thing but turning your axe on other people was something he didn't think he could do. Not in cold blood, not when they didn't have the chance to fight back.

He'd been welcomed into Krakenhom with the same hospitality he found anywhere else, disinterest and malaise. The world was not a welcoming place. And a sell-sword fresh off the path was not often wanted. People like him were seen as troublemakers. They dragged dust from the road and other terrible things with them. He took a room at an inn and decided that his stay in the tiny hamlet would be short lived. But the Burgomaster had other plans.

He was stout and fat, his beard a ragged mess of knots and crumbs. One leg had been separated under the knee. He walked on a peg, the broken wood shaft long cracked. His balance came from an equally worn cane. His name was Ilen and he spoke with the deep, ragged voice of a man who made proclamations, but did little to support them. Krakenhom was not a bad place, nor was it good. Duval had seen many like it, many unlike it. He thought little of Ilen.

Ilen, though, thought of him. Or, at least, what he could get from him. Sell-swords were not common in the valleys. They did not choose to walk among the peasants that scraped by on the land's meager offerings. When one was sighted, though, he was often the subject of many proposals. Most of the offers were foolish. Wasted time. Missing person contracts that would yield nothing but emptiness. A corpse if there was hope. But there was very little hope.

The Burgomaster came with a different proposition. Something more along Duval's experience. So, when the stout man sauntered into the inn and took a seat across from him, Duval chose to listen as opposed to pulling his axe.

He was told a tale. A good one, in fact. Krakenhom was founded by miners during the old age, before the sky went gray and the water black. In their mines, they pulled great ores. Sweet, beautiful rocks that could be refined into trinkets, weapons, jewelry. The finery that the few aging aristocrats so relished. It made Krakenhom a place of trade. They dug deep into the mines and people would come from across the valleys, from the ragged coast to collect what they found inside of their treasured mountains. For a time, the town thrived. Then, like all things, the prosperity turned to ruin.

The cataclysm. The darkened sky, the great cold, and the black water. The curse of the world. The end always coming but never present. The ore lost its sheen. The shine was gone and so too were the customers so willing to trade for the wonderful stones. The mine closed. The town fell into disarray and the great ruining settled here, as it did all places. As it always would.

But Ilen knew of one remaining stone. Far beyond the forest, along the Black River. The last member of Krakenhom's founding family, a man in power far before Ilen, had fled the town and sought out a fate made of more than ruin. He took with him the final stone pulled from the mine. The Hand. Named for its shape. The final shining stone, the last signal of Krakenhom's glory. And, of course, there was more to the story. The absconded townsman found himself in a deep cave hiding from the rain. As he settled, he was besought by a terrible brute. The man was killed, the Hand taken, and Krakenhom's history forgotten. Get it for me, Ilen said. Retrieve the Hand and he would make Duval a rich man.

Duval had learned to ask questions. He'd found himself lost in enough caves to know better. Not all treasure was worth seeking. Why had Ilen not sent men before? He had. Few returned. The ones that had, reported the beast unkillable. Why not go himself? Ilen pointed to his peg leg and laughed, wondered how he'd fair against a beast. What makes this time different? Ilen had learned the nature of the guardian. It was a troll. If they knew the monster, then it could be slain.

Duval nodded and dismissed himself from the table. He came back to the Burgomaster the next day and asked for half the payment up front and an herb-master. Ilen accepted the offer. And Undvik and Keir were summoned. The old man and his son were excitable. Herbalists weren't meant for the wild. They picked berries, crunched leaves, and burned strange mixtures. They often ruminated in their own fumes at things that others could not see. They were not made for a life on the road. Few were less prepared than the father and son presented to Duval. He took them nonetheless.

They'd made it most of the way to their destination by the time the boy was attacked. The party stopped at a ruined tower a quarter-day's walk from the Black River. Duval chose to follow the water. It provided the truest course. Whatever dim stars hung in the sky were obscured by the clouds. The river was long, looming. Strange things seemed to gravitate toward it. But it ran true. He kept the sound of the water on one ear and marched them forward.

They'd come up to a broken observation tower during their trek. It was cracked and leaning, but they believed that it to be sturdy. Duval checked the innards and found no one waiting in ambush. The stairs had long since rotted and broken. The sell-sword stared up the tower's length and saw no evidence of another being inside. They chose to camp within its walls, relieve themselves of the howling and trotting that came in the night. Perhaps even sleep well with a roof over their heads.

Kier was sitting by the fire when the thing came for him. Duval didn't know why the boy was chosen. It could have been his size. He was the smallest of them. Tall, but skinny. Easily moved by the wind. Or it could have been that he was seated too far from the fire. Maybe the flames would have offered him protection. In the end, it didn't matter. The beast chose him, and it is not often that a beast rethinks its choice.

It was winged, huge. Too large for the birds, bats, and owls that swooped in and out of the trees. The size of a man, its eyes wild with the firelight. It seemed to glow. Its gray feathers let off dust as it flapped its wings above them. The beast tore its talons into the meat between Kier's neck and shoulder. It hooked into his collarbone and pulled him first to his feet and then off them.

Undvik flew from his seat, he reached for his son's ankles. His fingers passed through air. His hands fell back to him empty. Duval, too, swung his axe at the thing. He tried not to hit Kier. In that, he was successful. He missed entirely. It flapped its great wings and carried the screaming boy to the top of the observation tower. They heard his screams quiet, as they were overtaken by sounds of slurping. Undvik cried at the base of the structure, he pounded his head into the stone until it bled.

Duval took to his pack. He pulled rope from it and began knotting it. The sling he made was sloppy. He found large rocks in the brush around them and gathered them in a small pile. The suckling was getting quieter. The beast was finishing its meal. Undvik cried in the background, forgotten.

The sell-sword took one of the rocks and secured it in the knot he fashioned. It sat well in place. Not bad for a hastily tied weapon in the dark. He swung the rope, the rock held, and he twisted his wrist to release. The missile flew from the sling and crack against the observation tower. Ancient bricks broke and rained down on the two men.

The beast was a pale outline in the dark. Duval tracked it by sound. The firelight offered little visibility. He focused on the creature and shot again. The rock missed. He pulled one more from the pile and flung it into the inky darkness. It hit. The creature didn't stagger or fall. The dull thud thumped the beast. It dropped Kier. The body fell, a used lump of flesh.

The thing swooped on Duval. Its talons came first, the wings at its side guiding its descent. He pulled the axe from his belt and shot the broad side of the blade in front of him, parried the talons aside. The creature continued past him, hit the ground ass first. It scuttled on the earth before gaining its footing. Its wings fanned on either side as its knuckled hands walked across the ground. Sharp fangs jutted out from a misshapen head. Duval thought that it could have been human once, but he made no assumptions. He only wished it death.

It lunged. The knuckles dug into the dirt and propelled it forward. The fanged mouth open and ready to clamp down on another piece of flesh. Duval swung the axe back, up, and down. The same motion he used to cut heavy logs into firewood. His aim was true. The blade stuck between the beast's eyes. The skull was cleaved to the fanged teeth. The force of the thing flung him backward. The strange corpse laid on top of him, trapping him below its leathery wings.

Undvik was no help. Duval pushed the beast from him. They would burn the corpse, lest it spawn from the dead and seek vengeance. Before they could do anything, Duval needed to pull Undvik from his son's corpse.

"No...no...no." Undvik was trying to feed Kier herbs from his pack. He pulled out a liquid concoction and poured it into his son's mouth. The corpse did not drink.

The boy was covered in his own blood. Some of it had come from the talons. The rest had leaked out of the great gouge pulled from his neck. The flesh was torn and bitten. The veins and arteries hung from the wound like drained worms.

It took the sell-sword a long time to calm the old man. Death was inevitable. The boy's end would have come eventually. Undvik had been unlucky enough to have witnessed it. He would move on. He had no choice. At least, that is what Duval told him. Whatever peace it brought him was unknown. But it was enough to convince the herb-master to help dig Kier's grave, to pull the beast's corpse onto the fire.

Though Kier rotted in the ground and the winged beast was nothing but crumbled ash, the journey continued. The cave, the Hand, and the troll. The coins that Ilen had given Duval clinked inside of his pocket. He'd been paid less for more and thought that perhaps he should count himself lucky. The thought passed quickly.

"How far?" Undvik said from behind him.

The old man had not spoken since they had left Kier's grave. It startled the sell-sword. He turned to look at the herb-master. The lines on his face were deeper now. They would never leave him. He would feel this pain for the remainder of his life. It was a sad thing. Duval had pulled him into this journey. It had not been his fate.

"Not long if Ilen tells us the truth." Duval said, his fingers running along the axe head on his belt.

"He does." Undvik said. "Ilen cares deeply about the Hand. You are not the first to be sent for it."

"Perhaps, I will be the last."

"You were smart enough to bring me." Undvik said. "That alone will strengthen your chances."

Duval knew little of beasts. But he knew trolls. They were deeply powerful things. Often injured, very rarely were they slain. A troll could withstand nearly any wound. It endured poisons, burning, even drowning. And, when it was healed, it would grow in power. If Ilen had sent as many men as Duval thought, then the beast would be more formidable than anything he had faced.

But, like all things, trolls had a weakness.

It was a mixture of strange herbs pulverized and boiled into an oil. The viscous liquid would be spread along a blade. It would cleave through the troll's skin. It would even break through the hardened scar tissue. Undvik knew the mixture and he carried the ingredients in his bag. He would mix the concoction by the fire.

As the sun began to descend the dark sky, they made their camp. They avoided the roads for fear of roving bands. It made finding their campsite easy. They stopped in the first clearing they found. It was tight, not much more than a large space between three trees formed into a triangle. They would sleep on roots and their backs would ache in the morning, but they would be mostly shielded from the road.

Undvik started the fire, while Duval wandered into the woods for kindling. The Black River ran hard and fast not far from where they would sleep. It caused an eerie feeling in Duval's gut. He knew it was a trick of the water, it wasn't truly black. It had grown dark from the silt floating in it. But he had also been on the road enough to hear the strange noises that seemed to emanate from the riverside. Especially at night.

He noticed something else, too. A figure in the distance. Their camp was situated on an incline, they had been climbing out of the valley during their march. Now that they were high up, Duval could see something moving along their path. Far in the distance, but still coming. He would set watch tonight. He gathered his bundles of wood and returned to the clearing.

"Someone is following us," he said.

The old man looked up from the small fire that he'd built. His tinctures and tools in hand. He looked more frustrated than concerned. Undvik watched his son die in front of him. He'd been forced to continue the march despite the grief. A moment alone in his trade was the type of healing he needed. And, that too, had been disturbed.

"What is it?" He said.

"I don't know. But I will sit watch tonight."

"It may not find us."

"It follows our path."

"Many things follow paths once they are cleared. That does not mean that it is following us. It may see the firelight and be warded off."

"You have high hopes for a man who has lost."

"I have only what it is left of me."

Pity flared in Duval and died out slowly. It was better to avoid friendship. He would not be making his roots in Krakenhom, nor did he plan to return. The Hand was a contract. It would be completed. He would move on. The world was a cracked and broken place. He would not spend his time scrounging together a life in a hovel hoping that tedium would save him from the cataclysm. The darkness was always encroaching. Duval thought it better to stay ahead of it.

He watched the herb-master working. His old hands moved in muscle memory. He crushed his leaves with a mortar and pestle, ground them down to a fine powder. Then, when that work was done, he boiled the black water from the river. The silt would need to be separated before it could be of use. It would take a long time to distill.

"You have an expert hand." Duval said. He'd pulled his axe from his belt and was running his travelling stone across the edge. The blade sung out with each pass of the rock.

"I have practiced since I was a child." Undvik continued crushing various herbs, as the black water cooked. "I taught Kier these things and it made me better at them. To teach is to learn, I suppose."

Duval watched the man, waited for him to descend into mourning. The herb-master was a good travelling companion. But he could become a burden. The loss of his son could put both their lives at risk if Undvik could not control his suffering. Undvik noticed the stare.

"It does me good to talk of him beyond his death. He is...was my son. And my memories of him will not be his death. They will be his life."

Undvik poured some of the purified water into the crushed herbs. He'd mixed the pulverized plants with his fingers. It produced a dark, sticky paste.

"He was eager to learn. Took it in easily. Categorizing, noting. This is the work of the herb-master."

"Not experimentation? Not strange vapors made to turn men's minds?" Duval said.

"No. Those are songs sung by bards to full bars of drunken men. These are plants, yes. But they are also chemicals. They are not to be taken lightly. The smallest mushroom I have discovered has enough poison inside it to kill an entire village. Crush it, slip it into a well. They will fall dead by the next day. The world we live in is unassuming. These plants look harmless, but they carry great secrets."

"And the oil to kill the troll?"

"It is something simpler than you would think. Quicksilver. Moonroot. Dried poison ivy. Crushed, mixed, kneaded into a paste and then cooked down into an oil. Simple. To us, nothing but a rash. Maybe an ill stomach should we drink it. To a troll, it is death."

"We will hope that it is death." Duval said.

"It will be." The old man turned his hand in the mixture. The lumpy goo began to smooth out. Duval could see the quicksilver running through it. The shining strands looked like veins in the paste. "And what of you, sell-sword?"

"What of me?"

"You come from the road, take sojourn in Krakenhom, and find yourself in the midst of Ilen's failed quest."

Duval turned his axe and began work on the opposite side. The small fire crackled. He pulled dried meat from his bag, tossed some to the herb-master.

"A mercenary is not often left to rest. My respite is often disturbed."

"And why do you bend to their wants?"

Duval considered it for a moment. He'd not often thought of his work. It was beyond him to consider the implications of his actions. He was hired, he did what was asked. Between the beginning and the end, there were scruples. There were lines he tried not to cross. Though, when it was summed up before him, it was simple. His axe was for hire. Only the price changed.

"A mercenary is surrounded by hungry, insatiable mouths." Duval said. "I feed those that I can."

"You make it sound virtuous." Undvik said.

"It is not."

"Then why do you continue?"

"I have practiced since I was a child."

Undvik stopped kneading the paste and looked up at Duval. His eyes narrowed, scrutinized. When he found no jest, his gaze lightened. A sympathy washed over the herb-master. Such things were known, but not often said. Fate is not something shared. As Undvik's hands were trained to carefully pluck leaves from stems, Duval's were made to swing swords. The world beckoned to be fed. They both sated the hunger in their own way.

They passed the night exchanging small conversation. Undvik finished the oil and presented it to the mercenary. The herb-master even took a short watch to allow his companion some rest. The night passed without incident. The follower did not come upon them in the night. When Duval checked the path from the top of the hill, he saw no sign of their stalker. The sell-sword was uneasy. But he was often uneasy, so he chose not to stall their mission. He gathered his things, the herb-master, and took to the Black River. The cave was along the water and he assumed they would reach it by midday.

He was wrong. The riverside became wild. They spent their morning trudging along the soft banks. The mud sucked at their shoes, the dewy fog seemed unwilling to abate. Duval thought that their journey could only get better. It didn't.

By midday they were beset by foliage that crowded around the river. They crawled through bushes and brambles, trees that leaned toward the dark water. There were no animal paths to follow. Nothing but the wild flora. They tried to track inland, found the forest so thick that Duval feared they would end up lost. They continued along the water. The branches and thorns tore at their skin and Duval wished for the mud, the slop, and the wet.

It was a good sign, though. The absence of other animals meant that they had entered the troll's territory. The beast was rumored to have won a hundred battles. At least, that was what Ilen had said and Undvik seemed to agree. That meant that it was huge, powerful, and often hungry. The troll had hunted this area of land and left nothing to trim down the vicious plants that surged in its wake. So, they continued. Undvik complained little. It was a stark contrast to the sell-sword's curses at each thorn that pricked him. By the time they found the cave, Duval had cursed nearly every plant, thorn, and branch along their way.

The path endured; they reached their destination before nightfall.

"It is terrible." Undvik said.

Duval agreed.

The cave was carved into a rocky hillside. The troll's home was next to the rumbling water. The entrance was huge. Perhaps it was natural or maybe the beast had bashed the rock open to make room. The opening rivaled some of the tallest trees in the forest. It was deep, dark, and seemed endless from the edge of the woods. He and Undvik hunkered down to survey the clearing.

The troll had scoured the area surrounding the cave. Though they were savage creatures, trolls were known to nest. Their homes were cleaned and ornamented. When they settled, they often did not leave. And this troll seemed to have settled ages ago.

It had adorned its yard with bones. The remaining skeletons of its attackers picked clean and shoved into the ground to make a fence. Femurs and humeri as the posts, the rest strung between them as the slats and lattice. Some had grown over with moss. Others were still fresh, the blood not yet washed off from the rain.

It had stacked clothes and armor near the cave's mouth. The discarded clothing seemed nearly as tall as Duval's waste. Helmets, chain mail, flails, swords, axes. Nothing now but toys to a beast that seemed to have toppled everything foolish enough to attack it.

"It seems Ilen was not the only one looking for the Hand."

"What do we do?" Undvik said, fear already beginning to emanate from his voice.

"We wait." Duval said. "Trolls are nocturnal. It won't emerge until night."

"But we have the oil. Why don't you go into its cave? Attack it while it sleeps?"

Duval stepped back from the edge of the clearing and found a space to set down his supplies. He pulled his axe from his belt and checked the blade. Though it was sharp, he could think of nothing but to pull the stone from his bag and run it along the steel's edge.

"Trolls make a home for themselves. They seldom leave it." Duval said. "Think of the spider, herb-master. When a fly is caught in its web, the spider feels the vibrations and races toward the prey. The troll is no different. If I took a step into that cave, it would know. It would feel the vibrations in the ground and be on me before my eyes adjusted to the dark."

Undvik found his own space and pulled out his mobile laboratory. He began pulling at jars instinctually. Duval noticed his hands shaking.

"Perhaps all of these fallen hunters chose to enter the cave." Undvik said.

"Perhaps."

"And that means that you may have a chance still."

"*We* may have a chance still." Duval said. "We are tied together in this thing, herb-master. I don't fancy your chances of making it back to Krakenhom without me to guide you."

"Nor do I." Undvik said, as he mixed another strange concoction in the waning light.

When the world was left in darkness. They heard the troll before they saw it. It lumbered through its cave, bashing along the sides as it made its way through the tunnels. Given the time the troll had lived there, it must have dug out endless amounts of paths into the rock. It was another reason Duval chose not to enter the lair. The troll could have carved a labyrinth into the hill.

"Take this." Undvik said.

The herb-master handed him a handful of wet, muddled herbs. Duval retracted from the scent.

"It will help you. It stalls pain."

"How?" Duval said.

"Eat it." Undvik said. He began packing up his mobile laboratory. "I have no way back to Krakenhom without you. It is not poison. The beast comes. I aim to heighten your chances of survival. I hope to see my son's grave again on our return."

Duval nodded. The beast's approach grew louder. He could hear it lumbering across the cave. It would emerge in moments. The sell-sword needed to move fast. Trolls, while often believed to be foolish, had a keen sense of smell and were skilled hunters. They noticed foreign scents on the wind. Its defenses would be up from the moment it stepped from the cave, if not sooner.

Duval ate the stinking mixture that Undvik handed him. It was sweet at first and then deeply bitter. It slid down his throat like a slug. It coated his stomach, emanated a cold from inside of him. His limbs felt numbed. He pulled his axe, could still feel. But he believed that if he was sliced open it would take a long time for the pain to register. It would have to do.

He slathered the edge of the blade in the oil. He'd sharpened the edges as well as he could. The oil would cleave the skin, the blade itself would need to do the damage. His old steel was strong. He hoped it would be strong enough to cut the troll's bones, its organs. Nothing was weak in a troll.

"Go." The herb-master said.

Duval rushed out from their cover. He knelt low to the ground and moved quickly, near silent. He'd scanned the cave often since they arrived and learned the layout. There was an outcropping of stone near the edge of the cave's opening. He thought that he could attack from above. Come down with a slashing blade and sever something from the beast's body. He'd mapped his climb and memorized the hand and footholds. The climb, though, was perilous. He stashed the axe into his belt and began. The stones were smaller than he thought. They barely jutted from the rock face, and he found his feet slipping, failing to gain purchase on the slick stone.

As he was halfway up the climb and still trying to gain footing, the troll emerged from its cave. It was a great beast. The height of two men. Nearly as wide as tall. It walked on over-large knuckles. Fingers the width of saplings curled upwards. Its body was covered in scars, weapons were embedded into the skin. Axes, swords, daggers, and knives. Most of the weapons were broken, the handles snapped. The sharp edges failed to breach all the layers of flesh and remained lodged inside of the troll. Where the cuts healed, the skin would be like stone. The beast's resilience would have increased with each scratch. Duval looked down in disbelief at the monster before him. He scrambled to reach the outcropping above the cave.

The troll sniffed at the air. It noticed the unfamiliar scent the moment it entered the clearing. For a second, he thought of the herb-master. He hoped that the old man had sought cover prior to the fight. He'd forgotten to warn Undvik. It didn't matter now. There was no time left.

It sniffed the air again and turned. As it looked about toward the cave, its grotesque eyes met Duval's. In strange ways, it looked like a man. It had ears, nose, eyes, and mouth. Though the tusks that jutted from under its upper lip resembled the jungle cats of the north. Drool dripped from its lips. It smelled of rot and shit. Its scent wafted over Duval as he stood waiting for the right moment.

The troll roared at him and he was greeted with its breath, a damp, putrid stench that nearly knocked him over. It reared back on of its gnarled hands and punched the space where he had been standing. Axe in hand, he came down at the troll. He maintained eye contact with it as he flew and slammed the oiled blade into the monster's face. The axe sliced the flesh clean, skidded along the bone, and the blade buried deep into its neck.

Duval landed on the troll's chest and began trying to wrench the axe from the beast's face. He had missed the brain. He'd hoped to end the battle with one stroke. But his axe had glinted off the skull and traveled diagonally down through the troll's eye and cheek. The skull was harder than he had anticipated. He pulled the weapon free before the troll could react. He did not have time for a second swing.

The beast howled in anger and agony. Its gnarled maw swept into Duval's shoulder. The sell-sword flew from the beast's chest and bounced off the ground. The compacted rock and dirt gave no cushion. He saw black flashes in his vision before he felt his nearly numb limbs crying out in pain. The herb-masters decoction was not enough to stall the crunch of broken ribs. Duval sucked in a labored breath as he tried to lift himself from the ground. The axe skittered on the stone and landed out of sight.

As the troll loomed over him, Duval wondered what he would number for the beast. Maybe in the hundreds now. The thing would live on again. It would crush more mercenaries and, maybe, it would never be stopped. The world would continue to degrade, and the troll would live on.

Infinite, even as the great fires scorched the earth and the blackened ash rained down.

Undvik's vial hit the beast on the back of the head. If Duval had not cleaved off part of its face, the troll may not have noticed. But the liquid inside of the glass container dripped down into the wound and the monster grabbed at the flayed skin, pulling the flesh as though tearing it away would stop the pain. Smoke bloomed from the wound. It smelled chemical and sinister.

Duval took the time to come to his feet and find his axe. It laid unbroken in the brush off the side of the troll's clearing. He turned to find the enemy locked in battle with itself. The facial wound was smoking. The troll was tearing the skin away, hoping that it would stop the pain. It wouldn't.

Duval ran. The axe was still coated in the oil. The numbing agent had found purchase in his blood again. The ribs seemed like a distant pain, a bruise. He would overcome it, power through. With his feet under him, he lifted his axe and drove it deep into the troll's stomach. He hooked the edge of the blade under the flesh and began tearing. Vile, black blood flooded from the deep wound, as he yanked at the thing's innards.

Even with the stone-like scar tissue, the axe cut cleanly. A sharp butcher's knife through flesh. Entrails fell from the wound and slopped onto the ground in front of the mercenary. He tore the axe from the viscera and reared back for another cut.

The troll had stopped worrying about the burning acid on its face and looked down to find his adversary bathing in its own blood. Its torn, ruined countenance stared at Duval with a grim sadness that the sell-sword did not expect. While it glared at him, Duval drove the axe into its side. Like a stuck pig, the blackened blood flooded out easier now that it was uncorked. The troll lifted its arms to smash the attacker. Its movements were slow, drained of malice. The mercenary jumped back. Its fists smashed the ground.

Duval backed away. He stowed his axe in his belt. It was no longer needed. He put an arm across his broken ribs and then took a seat on one of the rocks that surrounded the troll's clearing.

The beast balanced on its knuckles and then sunk slowly to the ground. Its breath was labored, it looked tired. The dozens of weapons stuck in its skin rose and fell with its breath, until they no longer moved. The beast looked to be sleeping. If it was not surrounded by its own blood and organs it would have looked at peace.

The herb-master approached carefully. Duval waved him forward. He had his mobile laboratory on his back. He carried an extra vial in hand.

"A hard death." Undvik said.

"No harder than it had given to those before us." Duval said.

"And the Hand?"

"Around its neck." Duval pointed to the string that hung loose from the troll's chest. "Thank you, herb-master."

"I told you that you were smart to bring me. I felt the need to prove it to you."

"Consider it proven."

Duval rose, the pain beginning to show itself now. He would be banged up and bruised. His ribs would need to be wrapped. He figured that the herb-master could help him. At least long enough to get a surgeon to look at him. But it would have to wait. The journey before them was still long. And he would need to return the old man to Krakenhom.

He pulled the Hand from the troll's neck. The beast was gone now, slayed finally. The hand was an ugly thing. It was missing fingers and the crooked digits that remained were stuck clenching the air. It was the size of his own hand. He set the prize in his pack. It was his now. That and half the payment from Ilen.

He planned to tell the herb-master before they returned to Krakenhom. There was no doubt that Ilen would punish Undvik if he did not return with the Hand. But Duval had no intention of relinquishing the artifact. Not when so many were after it, not when it could fetch a higher price. Ilen had not inspired loyalty. Not with the many men that he had sent to their deaths. Not with his peg leg and his questionable smile, his deals and greasy handshake. No. Ilen would never see the treasure he so cherished. But that did not mean that Undvik deserved punishment. Duval planned to ask the herb-master to join him. For a time, at least. There were other towns in need of his herbs and remedies. Kier was dead and, perhaps, the old man would value a new home.

He turned to find the herb-master gone. He searched the clearing and found no sign of him. Then he spotted Undvik near the woods. Something was approaching from the brush. He was on the edge of the clearing. He was walking right toward it.

Duval remembered something had been following them. He watched it from the high hill along the Black River. He'd forgotten it after their night passed without incident. The troll had taken his attention.

He pulled the axe from his belt. His arms were heavier now. The fight had taken it out of him. The manic energy of blood and pain was gone. A malaise was coming over him, as it did all those who had faced death and lived.

He fought exhaustion and strode toward the herb-master's side. He was not halfway there when he saw what had emerged from the trees. It was Kier. The flesh taut over the bone, the blood still drained from his body. He had begun to decay. His eyes had popped and sunk into his skull. The shambling corpse moved without grace. It bumped against trees, walked through bushes. But it followed their path. It sought them out.

The herb-master's voice broke as he tried to speak. The cracked whimper escaped his lips and died in the air. Undvik walked toward the corpse. His steps mirrored Kier's. Slow, plodding. The old man did not have the strength to run. His eyes were trained on his son and he walked to him with open arms.

"Undvik." Duval said.

The herb-master continued. His shambling walk now straightening. The realization that he would hold his son again allowed his remaining strength to blossom. Kier, as though he recognized the old man, held out his own arms to embrace his father. Undvik walked into them openly.

Duval found himself running. The axe was pulled back, ready to strike the corpse. He watched as the living dead thing took the herb-master into its arms and held tight. A hug that Undvik would have enjoyed if the boy had not opened his stiff jaw and clamped his teeth down into the old man's neck. Blood spurted out of the wound. Undvik screamed, but it was drowned out by the sound of the corpse sucking on the blood. The air between its teeth was a whistle. The warm liquid slid down the corpse's throat and, near immediately, its pallor, drained complexion began to improve.

The herb-master was in the way. Duval pivoted to the side and smashed the axe into the corpse's back. The thing did not shudder, nor scream. It raised its head again and bit down into the old man's flesh. Blood spurted, less now. Undvik made no sound. His face was buried in his son's neck. Though the boy smelled of the earth and rotting flesh, his father would not turn away.

Duval pulled the axe from the dead body and raised it over his head. He smashed it down into the back of the thing's skull. His muscles twinged and barked at him. The exhaustion running through him made his eyes burn at their edges. But the blade found purchase. It smashed through the back of Kier's skull and cracked the bone up to the now-empty eye sockets. The corpse was nearly decapitated from the nose up. Its grip failed. The herb-master fell to the ground with the corpse. They piled on top of each other. Duval sheathed the axe in his belt and knelt to the old man.

"What have you done?" Undvik said.

His face was the same as Kier's when he died. The skin white and sick. He'd been drained. Not completely, but enough blood was gone to make his flesh cold. The skin was close to the bone and it made the herb-master look more like a bag of bones than a man.

"Killed my boy again," he said. "Killed him again."

He stroked the corpse that had fallen on top of him. Kier's skull was in Undvik's lap. He stroked the sparse hair, as his neck continued to bleed.

"Leave us," he said.

"Undvik."

"Leave me with my son. It's you that killed him the first time and now again." Undvik's eyes looked toward him. It would not be long now. "We have done what we were to do. We are through."

Duval smelled the iron scent as he stood. He waited for the old man to die. It took minutes. When his blood had gone cold and there was nothing left but the running water in the Black River, Duval burned the bodies. He left to troll to rot in the open. The animals would return to feed on its corpse and the once abandoned area of the woods would be populated again. Until the world crashed, until the darkness overtook all, and the sun refused to rise.

The Hand glowed a deep crimson in the diffuse daylight. It was the brightest thing that Duval had ever seen. He hid it deep in his pack, lest someone else should see its beautiful light.

Who?

A Jersey girl at heart, when **Lisa Voorhees** is not writing, she's usually listening to hard rock, bouldering, or sipping amaretto sours. Before she started writing novels, she earned her doctorate in veterinary medicine from Tufts University. Find out more about her at https://lisa.voorhe.es or http://facebook.com/lisavoorheesauthor . Interested in becoming a patron? Find out more about how to support her creative work and receive bonus material at http://www.patreon.com/lisavoorhees .

Ethan Robles is a writer working out of Boston, MA. His fiction has appeared in the *NoSleep Podcast, Guilty Crime Story Magazine, Aphotic Realm,* and *Shotgun Honey.* You can follow him on Twitter @roblecop. More at ethanrobles.com.

Jason Lairamore is a writer of science fiction, fantasy, and horror who lives in Oklahoma with his beautiful wife and their three monstrously marvelous children. He is a published finalist and a third place winner in the *SQ Mag* contest. He has won honorable mention thirteen times and Semi-Finalists once in the *Writers of the Future* contest. His work is both featured and forthcoming in over 100 publications to include *Neo-Opsis*, New Myths, *Stupefying Stories*, and Third Flatiron publications, to name a few.

Lisa Timpf is a retired HR and communications professional who lives in Simcoe, Ontario. When not writing, Lisa enjoys organic gardening, bird watching, and taking long walks with her cocker spaniel-Jack Russell mix Chet. Lisa's speculative fiction has appeared in *NewMyths,Home for the Howlidays, Cosmic Crime*, and other venues. Lisa's collection of speculative haibun poetry, *In Days to Come*, is available from Hiraeth Publishing. You can find out more about Lisa's writing at http://lisatimpf.blogspot.com/.

Angela Acosta is a bilingual Latina poet and scholar from Gainesville, Florida with a passion for the distant future and possible now. She is a member of the Science Fiction Poetry Association, and her speculative poetry has appeared in *Altered Reality Magazine, Eye to the Telescope, MacroMicroCosm*, and *Radon Journal*. Angela won the 2015 Rhina P. Espaillat Award from West Chester University for her Spanish poem "El espejo". She received BA degrees in English Language and Literature and Spanish from Smith College and an MA in Spanish from The Ohio State University where she is completing a PhD in Iberian Studies. Her academic articles and translations have appeared in *Ámbitos Feministas, El Cid, Metamorphoses*, and *Persona Studies*. Her creative and academic work center on imagining possible worlds and preserving the cultural legacies of minoritized writers. This is Angela's first poetry collection.

www.ingramcontent.com/pod-product-compliance
Lightning Source LLC
LaVergne TN
LVHW012028060526
838201LV00061B/4514